WE'RE NOT HERE

For almost 20 years, psychologist G. Robert "Bob" Baker counseled combat veterans and medical personnel who served in Vietnam and other wars. Dr. Baker served in combat in Vietnam in 1965-66.

Over the years, he acquired a sizeable collection of war-related books from authors, fellow clinicians and veterans.

Dr. Baker has generously donated this treasured book to the General Ames Library.

Semper Fidelis, Dr. "Bob"   August 2000

By the same author

HOLLARAN'S WORLD WAR

WE'RE NOT HERE
NOT HERE
TIM MAHONEY

Published by
Dell Publishing
a division of
The Bantam Doubleday Dell Publishing Group, Inc.
666 Fifth Avenue
New York, New York 10103

Library of Congress Cataloging in Publication Data
Mahoney, Tim.
    We're not here / Tim Mahoney.
      p. cm.
    ISBN 0-440-55004-1
      1. Vietnamese Conflict, 1961–1975—Fiction.
I. Title.
   PS3563.A377W4   1988   88-3943
813'.54—dc19   CIP

Manufactured in the United States of America
November 1988

10 9 8 7 6 5 4 3 2 1

BG

This novel is dedicated to the memory
of Kevin Francis Mahoney
and Sergeant John Service
and others who couldn't make it home

Contents

WE'RE NOT HERE

Xin Loi
1982

Bill Lemmen walks the dirtier streets of San Francisco, looking only at Asian faces. He's the kind of white man who can tell at a glance: Chinese from Korean, Thai from Viet, Filipino from Cambodian. Once, maybe twice, in a day's walking Lemmen will stop, transfixed by the face of a passing man or, more usually, woman. Sometimes he'll follow them a short way; he's so big, so shabbily dressed that the woman might cut across the street or the man might stop and turn. Then Lemmen will retreat a step. "Excuse me," he'll say, and make the beginnings of a bow. *"Xin loi."*

These days it is winter, bay fog and high clouds, and Lemmen walks the Tenderloin, that ghetto for refugees from the world's lost causes. Lemmen has the remnants of a crisp, arm-swinging walk; he's dressed in a faded army jacket, an outline of stripes on the sleeves.

Near Eddy and Larkin it looks like another nation: derelict apartment buildings, chaotic grocery stores, grimy restaurants serving thin customers, newsstands full of foreign headlines. The language is shrill and nasal; the streets smell of vegetables, fish, sewage, rice, flowers.

Lemmen pauses in a grocery doorway; inside, a gray-haired woman, her hair pushed into a bun, is bent over stacking sacks of rice. He pushes through the door. "Yes?" the woman says, and looks up.

"Can I look around?" he asks.

An annoyed look takes over the woman's face. She stares at the door as if something's wrong with it.

"Oh, you're not really open, are you?" Lemmen says. He glances around. Never can tell who might be stocking the shelves, sweeping the floor. But in here, nobody. He nods and tries to smile at the woman. *"Xin loi ba,"* he says.

The woman goes back to stacking rice sacks and Lemmen is out on the street again. Around the corner he stops to look over a menu taped in a window. Not that he's hungry—this place, the Sunflower, has just been renovated. It has been fixed up very nicely, considering the neighborhood. The interior is expensive blond wood, trimmed with yellow. The sunflower-shaped menu describes fancy, spicy lunches that start at seven dollars. Lemmen shakes his head. Nothing on the menu is familiar at all.

He walks into another small grocery, his first time in here. Glances at the owner: a man in his thirties, thick eyeglasses, round-faced, a Chinese. Lemmen nods a greeting and prowls the narrow aisles. He's the size of a bull in these aisles. Surrounded by packages of lichee nuts, bottles of soyu, chili water, *nuoc-mam*. He takes his time. Drifts into the section of rice cookers, stacked bowls, rusting woks. A tiny old woman comes into the store and talks in the only foreign language Lemmen even dimly understands. The talk seems to be about a family named Dong, Lemmen gets that much. The Dongs' daughter is turning out to be a problem. She is crazy about American boys. Lemmen picks up a plate, there's a painting of a bird on it, a bird on a bamboo limb. Lemmen pretends to inspect the plate and listens, trying to pick out words he understands.

He'll always buy something in a store like this. When the old woman finally leaves, Lemmen takes his plate to the cash register. The grocer smiles and punches in the price. Strictly a merchant's smile.

"Where are you from?" Lemmen asks, and hands over a dollar and change.

"Pardon me?"

"What town are you from?" He does not want to add *over there*. He has learned not to be too pushy.

"I do not understand," the shopkeeper says.

Lemmen says it slowly: "Where did you live?"

"Richmond," the man says. Struggles a little with the *R*.

"No, I mean before that," Lemmen says.

"Hong Kong," the man says. Lemmen stares at the man, and a foreign word, *xau*, almost escapes his lips.

"Oh, Hong Kong," Lemmen says. "And before that?"

"Hong Kong," the man insists.

Lemmen nods. Enough Oriental has seeped into his mind and heart; he understands the lie and its necessity. He takes the plate, refuses a bag, thanks the shopkeeper. *"Cam on ong,"* he says, and watches for a reaction. But the shopkeeper doesn't even blink.

Outside, carrying his plate, Lemmen looks up and down the street. At one time a disappointment would have sent him into the nearest dark hole for a drink. But there have been too many disappointments, and too many drinks, and now Lemmen is a coffee man. Coffee and long walks.

Block after block he keeps walking, past refugees and the homegrown drifters, druggies, runaway teenagers, winos, whores, spare-change artists. Lemmen has a certain sympathy for these people; he knows that a small guaranteed pension is the basic difference between him and them. If he has a little extra money, he'll sometimes give it away, but never with the illusion of its doing any good.

He turns a corner and heads into the gleaming part of

the city. Today he is forty years old. He is still too heavy from his drinking days. He needs a shave and maybe a shower.

He walks the streets like a bum in combat boots. A very tall, dark-haired bum, with a thick black mustache. He gets to the wider, cleaner sidewalks of Union Square, passes theaters and airline offices, palm trees planted in cement pots, department stores with beautiful manne-quins in the windows. Now he's among stockbrokers and bankers, secretaries and office boys, shoppers from the suburbs, lawyers and accountants—all those bright Amer-ican faces, salmon-colored shirts, pinstriped suits; every-body in a hurry, even the women wearing ties. To Lem-men these people seem foolish; they are order takers, all of them, and headed for doom. This he knows! Look at them, they're as much in uniform, as much on the march, as anyone in the military.

Lemmen turns toward Chinatown, then takes a shortcut to North Beach. In an alley is a smoky bar, crowded at midday, a stool keeping the door open, a scratchy "Satis-faction" blasting from a jukebox. Lemmen stops and lis-tens as the famous raspy singer says he tried, tried, tried. He sees, on the barstools, bitter-thin men, not young any-more, the remnants of Thieu's army, dressed in T-shirts and shiny pants. A glare from a scarred and pitted face makes Lemmen keep walking.

He's come almost full circle now, just up the hill from the pyramid skyscraper, the top of it lost in fog. He walks uphill past Italian restaurants, coffeehouses named for op-eras, marquees promoting sex shows. At a check-cashing place, he stops at a smudged window; it's like looking through a dirty cloud. The clerk does business from a gun slot, behind dark bulletproof glass, transactions recorded by a caged camera bolted to the ceiling. Lemmen finds himself staring at a woman, the only customer. She's an Asian, dressed in bright, cheap blue jeans and high-top sneakers—clothes bought on the other side. She sits waiting for something to be approved, hands in her lap, head down. She's about thirty years old, and something about her face is all Asia: scarred and anxious, tired and suspicious. Lemmen opens the door.

Inside, it reeks of sweat and cigarettes; the smell gags Lemmen now that he's quit the Lucky Strikes. He sucks in a shallow breath, sits in an orange plastic seat near the woman. Who looks toward the opposite wall. Lemmen realizes he's made a mistake, tries to fix it by staring away. Knows he must look like a crazy man; there's a plate in his hands. He stares at his boots, and between them the dirty tiles; he has a quick dream of monsoons and mosquitoes, rice paddies, straw houses, wide rivers, clusters of palm trees.

"Okay, miss!" shouts the clerk, and the woman walks to the slot and stands two feet back. All Lemmen can see of the clerk is his hands, counting greenbacks, pushing them through the slot. The woman folds the money into a change purse, slips it into the waistband of her jeans, pulls her white blouse out to cover it, walks for the door.

Lemmen gives her a moment, then follows. She looks over her shoulder only once, but after that walks faster and faster. Two blocks up the hill and she's nearly running; at the park, she boards a bus as its doors are closing. The bus moves a few feet, stops for a traffic light. Lemmen knocks on the door and it opens.

The woman is alone in the seat behind the driver, her arms folded over her waistband. Lemmen realizes how badly he's scared her; chooses a seat across the aisle. As the bus starts moving, the woman looks to the other passengers, most of them elderly Chinese, as if she's going to cry for help.

He puts the plate in his lap, brings out his wallet; from it he pulls a Xerox copy of a black-and-white photo. He leans into the aisle, tries to hand it to the woman, but she shakes her head, her arms wrapped tightly around her waistband.

"*Xin doc cai nay,*" Lemmen says. He turns the photo over, where, in block letters in two languages, are the words IF YOU HAVE SEEN THIS WOMAN PLEASE CONTACT S/SGT. WILLIAM E. LEMMEN, USA (RET) along with phone and post office box numbers. In bigger type is the word REWARD.

Finally the woman puts her hand out maybe two inches to take the picture. She looks at it, glances at Lemmen, then looks back at it. Typed under the picture are the words *Hoa Muon, Vinh Long, RVN.* The woman shakes her head, tries to give the picture back to Lemmen.

"Keep it," Lemmen says. "*Thuong.* Reward." The woman gives him a puzzled look, then stares down at her feet, and at the next stop Lemmen gets off.

He walks, holding his plate. He crosses Columbus against heavy traffic, legs it over the broad lawn of the park, past the statue of Ben Franklin, speckled with bird droppings, surrounded by sleeping bums. A block later Lemmen climbs a stairway that smells of garlic and mold, puts his hand on a cracked porcelain knob, opens the door on a room crowded with things from another world.

Asia picture calendars are tacked to the walls; plates and bowls are piled in one corner; end tables are crowded with little things: bronze statues, incense burners, ceramic monkeys, tigers, and elephants. Woks and bamboo steamers—overflow from the closetlike kitchen—sit under a carved coffee table. A straw sleeping mat covers the worn-out sofa, which sits next to a two-foot-high Buddha holding a begging bowl. In the Buddha's bowl are a Seiko watch and a gold crucifix on a gold chain.

He puts the plate down on a cardboard filing cabinet, the drawer pulled halfway out. It overflows with yellowed letters and replies: the Red Cross, the refugee commissions, newspapers in foreign cities. Lemmen tries to close the drawer with his foot, it's too heavy and too full. He takes off his jacket and hangs it on back of the door. He is in no mood to celebrate his birthday; maybe later he'll go out for cake and coffee; now he needs sleep. He lies on the couch, closes his eyes, and remembers another birthday, years ago and far away . . .

It was a land of elephants and tigers. It was a land of monkeys and snakes.

Operation Scarecrow
1975

Bill Lemmen looked over a wide river the color of creamed coffee. A sampan was floating upriver, an old papa-san in it waving. Lemmen strapped a canvas bag over his shoulder and waved back. He watched the boat—slow, sure, powered by nothing but tide—float toward the spot where the lowering sun would meet the palm trees.

Lemmen stood in the shade underneath Tower Nine for a moment, enjoying a breeze, his shirt open the regulation one button. He put his foot on the step of a wooden ladder and wiped sweat from his face with an olive-drab bandanna. Across the river were two houses: a damaged one of straw and bamboo, and a ruined one of stone. Lemmen stared at them and lit a Lucky.

The stone house must have been a beauty at one time, probably a landlord's place. There were still hints of floor tiles, bright blue, underneath the rubble. The roof had been blown away, and so had one wall, except for a chimney; the standing walls were singed, black over white. When Lemmen had come here on his first tour—six years before—the stone house was abandoned, but not damaged.

Lemmen had been surprised, on coming back for his second tour, by a lot of things—including the fact that the stone house had been destroyed, while the bamboo one stood—a testament to something, if he could only think what.

He flicked his cigarette out toward the river, adjusted the canvas bag, climbed the ladder. He pushed through the trapdoor and into a guard bunker with waist-high walls made of sandbags and railroad ties. Lemmen hoisted himself up, stood, dropped the bag on top of the wall, took a look at Lyndon and Dick. They were dummies Lemmen had made the week before, using sandbags and GI uniforms. Lyndon looked asleep, as ever, in a hammock, a helmet on his sandbag head, a faded uniform over his sandbag body. A pair of old combat boots hung over the edge of the hammock. The name tag on Lyndon's uniform said, in laundry marker: *Greetings.* Dick's said: *Goodbye.*

Dick was built just like Lyndon, only Dick wore smashed sunglasses and a boonie hat, and sat limp in a lawn chair behind a rusty machine gun mounted atop the wall. The gun was loaded with a starter belt of ammo, which fell away to nothing behind the wall. Lemmen pushed Dick's chair toward the corner. "Give you some sun," he said, and adjusted the dummy's boonie hat. He pointed the machine gun upriver, toward the swamp, toward the sun, toward Cambodia. Took his bayonet out, poked a hole where Dick's mouth would be, inserted a Lucky Strike. "Light 'em up if you got 'em," he said.

Lemmen looked upriver for that sampan, but it was out of sight—amazing how fast that could happen, but the Mekong's current only looked slow. If you actually got in the river, it was frighteningly fast, could suck a man downriver and ship him back with the next tide, a bloated purple log. Lemmen had seen that for himself, back on his first tour. Jimmy Carney was the guy's name.

Lemmen bent and picked up what he had come for: pop-flares, a dozen of them. In two big handfuls he dropped them into the bag, then climbed down the ladder, pulling the trapdoor shut over his head. He climbed a low sand dune and slid down its face, walked on the river side of it, his mind toning down thoughts of snipers. Not anymore, not in the daytime, he told himself.

Between him and the river lay a tangled thirty-foot-wide mess: barbed-wire fencing, rusty concertina wire, tripflares, and claymore mines, with beer and soda cans hung in pairs from the barbed wire. Lemmen walked the wire, checking for cuts, snips, tunneling, or tripflares that might have been disabled. At Tower Ten he squatted to pick up a claymore, the green plastic cover cracked by the weather, showing white explosive inside. The side that said FRONT TOWARD ENEMY was facing the wrong way. "Great," he said, and shook his head. He screwed out the blasting cap, a silvery firecracker attached to electric wires. Rolled the wires around the blasting cap, slipped it into his thigh pocket. Dropped the mine among others in the canvas bag. Front toward enemy. Simplest idea in the world, Lemmen told himself, but around Delta Town these days, no one could seem to grasp it.

He started walking again, passed Tower Eleven, scooped up two more claymores—it spooked him, to have the towers staffed by dummies, but even that was becoming normal. When he got to within a few feet of Tower Twelve, he started to feel better, seeing an Arvin soldier up there, along with Sergeant Nuong. He also felt worse, knowing that the soldier was a peasant boy more or less kidnapped off the streets by some desperate Arvin commander.

Well, Lemmen thought, at least the kid has a good teacher in Nuong. As soon as he thought that, he was surprised—Nuong whipped the boy with a cleaning rod. A smart smack right across the back, from which the kid didn't flinch. The boy tried to load the big machine gun, but his hands were shaking. Lemmen could almost feel the boy's pain, and felt sorry him—he was just a teenager, his

GI helmet far too big for him, coming down around his ears.

Lemmen was surprised because he had never known Nuong to be cruel. He climbed the dunes, held his arm up at an angle, and gave Nuong a wave, local style, hand dangling from the wrist. Nuong waved back with the cleaning rod. He smiled—briefly. "I will come—perhaps in a few minutes," Nuong called, and when he caught the boy looking at Lemmen and grinning, he whipped him on the shoulder.

Lemmen hesitated, then decided—better not to interfere. "I'll have a cold beer waiting for you," he shouted, and half walked, half slid down the side of the dunes; the canvas bag banged heavy against his hips, the river and the towers were behind him; what was left of Delta Town Army Airfield was in front of him. He walked toward the crossroads of it, along a hot, dusty, empty road.

He walked past a gun jeep, rusted, tires half rotted; past a dried-up pond once used as a fire-fighting reservoir; past a yard full of helicopters crashed into balls, shot to pieces, or ripped up for spare parts; past quiet barracks with doors left open, no one inside. At the last barracks, near the crossroads, he stopped, walked a metal plank over a smelly drainage ditch, and nudged the door open with his boot. All ghosts inside. Lemmen knew for sure there were such things as ghosts—they could belong to the spirits of the dead or the living. For instance: Buck, Carney, Bumstead, Dixon, Little Lloyd Little, Holloway. They'd all been Lemmen's men and now, dead or alive, they weren't here anymore, the big room was all folded mattresses, open lockers, mold, dustballs—ghosts.

He walked down the aisle, which was marked on the concrete floor with narrow white stripes almost lost in dust. Memories came back on him, too many to let any one in. He got to a small room built of plywood—it had been his room years ago and it was his again—and opened the plywood door on a single bunk, neatly made; a gray-metal

wall locker and a green wooden footlocker; two small fans;
a bank of military radios; and a small refrigerator. Lemmen dropped the canvas sack at the foot of his bunk. He
took the coils of wire, the blasting caps, and the clackers
out of his thigh pockets, piled them in one corner, far
away from the canvas bag. Then he dropped to one knee
and opened his footlocker. The first level was in top military order, with rolled-up socks, folded bandannas, a razor
turned blade down, shaving cream, toothpaste, a tooth-
brush and a bar of soap in their plastic containers, a round
mirror, malaria pills, shampoo. He lifted that level out:
beneath it was a mess of T-shirts, blue jeans, naked-girl
magazines, an electric football game, packs of Luckies, a
red transistor radio.

That was what he wanted. He picked up the radio,
turned it on to AFVN. It was playing one of the many
rock 'n' roll songs he didn't recognize. He left it turned on
—but not for the music. In the last weeks there had been
all kinds of rumors, each new one contradicting the last,
and it made him feel better to hear the American station.
GIs were still up there in Saigon, things were still okay,
and the broadcast was proof. He dropped the radio into
his shirt pocket, buttoned it in.

He left the barracks door open when he came out, and
walked toward the main gate. There wasn't one other soldier walking, wasn't a jeep or truck moving, no helicopters warming up on the runway. When he'd first seen this
base, helicopters and small planes were all over the runways; trucks and jeeps jammed the main roads, along with
a stream GIs on foot: mechanics, grunts, flyboys, cooks,
medics, and clerks—five thousand men, a magnificent
commitment. Just before Lemmen had arrived for that
first tour, the VC had launched a big Tet attack in the
Delta, and although they overran the base, blew up the
ammo dump, wrecked a lot of helicopters, and killed
twelve Americans, it cost them nearly every man they
had; the survivors had to flee for the Seven Sisters, where,

rumors said, they lived miserably on lizard meat and rice. At Delta Town Airfield, and in the little city of Vinh Long, the GIs and Arvins found themselves suddenly in charge; in the first months of Lemmen's tour they chased down a few exhausted, half-starved VC squads, and an occasional sniper, and soon, if not a ceasefire then at least the illusion of it came to the marketplaces, the streets, the alleys, the rice paddies, the hamlets, the canals, the rivers, the trails.

With peace, the town started to change. Bars and whorehouses were full of customers, peasants bought TVs, shopkeepers rode motorbikes. Up north, the radio said, a ferocious war still raged, but in Vinh Long, weeks could pass without a single gunshot.

Two months into that long lull Lemmen was leading his squad through the reedy swamp outside the airfield; it was daytime, they were searching for the place where, the night before, a VC had fired a single mortar round that had exploded harmlessly on a runway. They walked and walked, and trampled the reeds, but they knew they wouldn't find so much as a footprint. Buck Shannon, hung over as usual, wanted a break. They sat in a circle, behind a stand of reeds on the bank of a small stream, and three guys stood the first guard while the rest of them—Little, Bumstead, Buck, Lemmen—sat and drank from their canteens. Bumstead put the M-60 in his lap and lit a joint. Buck popped open a can of Miller High Life. Little turned his radio to AFVN, hoping for music, but he got the voice of the President of the United States. Who was saying something about the Delta! Lemmen shushed everyone. The president was telling some journalists that the war was won in the Delta, that the South Vietnamese could win without American help. He said there were no American combat soldiers in the Mekong Delta, and had not been any for months. Buck spat beer. Bumstead snorted and said, Those fucks. Little had a hurt look on his face. When the president stopped speaking, Lemmen said the

9th Cav had probably gotten lost in the bureaucracy; they weren't supposed to be here, the president had just said so, and they would be pulled out as soon as the army realized its mistake. Bumstead sputtered and blew out smoke. Buck said: You lie good, Lemmen, then put his head back and actually poured beer from the can into his throat.

But all that was six years ago—now things in the Delta were different again. There was hardly any fighting but business was bad. Bars, whorehouses, massage parlors, pool halls, barber shops, and food stands stood empty. The GIs were almost really gone—except for a few pilots, crew chiefs, and mechanics in Can Tho. At Delta Town the defenders were now Vietnamese, twenty or thirty old men, boys, and cripples guarding a base that once was its own small city.

Lemmen stopped to look back at the main crossroads: the church, the battalion mess hall, the post office—everything closed, a ghost town in olive drab. Lemmen stopped at the NCO club and looked in the window—they'd locked everything inside: stools, tables, the jukebox, and even some of the booze; the GIs had been in that much of a hurry to leave. He kept walking, past a mural painted on one side of his barracks, a big romantic painting that had been there for years, a scene in the Arizona desert: blue-uniformed men cooking at a campfire, their mounts tied nearby, a mountain range far behind them, a darkening sky. Lettered above the scene, in foot-high characters on a blue scroll, were the words

9th U.S. CAVALRY

Under which some wiseguy had scrawled in black spray paint:

WE'RE NOT HERE

Across an alley from that mural was Command's trailer, painted red, white, and blue in longitudinal thirds, and surrounded by sandbags piled two feet high. Lemmen stepped lightly in front of that trailer, with a feeling he was slinking. He hoped that if he walked gingerly enough, Command wouldn't look out the trailer window, wouldn't call his name, wouldn't give him any new orders for Operation Scarecrow.

He made the main gate, a high cyclone fence reinforced with sandbags and railroad ties, a machine-gun jeep parked just inside it, gun pointed out. Lemmen passed the guard shack, a passageway with just room enough for one person to squeeze out. He gave a salute to two sleepy Vietnamese QCs.

The moment he got outside, an old cyclo driver started his Honda and drove toward him; Lemmen knew better than to resist a ride, even though he was going just a few blocks. He hopped in the rickshaw seat; didn't have to call a destination, only one GI bar still open downtown. The cyclo started off, slow, noisy, leaking blue smoke, the old man leaning over the handlebars. Lemmen remembered when there might be fifty rickshaw-cyclos out there, the drivers swarming toward each emerging GI, frantic to earn a few piasters for the ride downtown.

Lemmen looked back at Delta Town, behind all its towers, its tons of sandbags, its miles of barbed wire. In a few hours, when the sun sank over Cambodia, timers would light up the empty barracks, blue lights would burn steady on unused runways, and over each tower, big sets of arc lights would hum and glow, hiding dummies, rusted guns, and nervous teenagers in their shadows.

Hoa Muon stood in front of a cracked, full-length mirror in white underpants, looking herself over. She was much too thin, she told herself. And her tiny breasts, there wasn't any hope for them. Her legs would always be bowed, and blotchy with faded circles of ringworm, and scarred with dark points of leech bites. She put her arms through the straps of a red bra and hooked it in back, bending her head with the effort. She took bobby pins out of her hair, let it down, played with it. Black, curly, and soft, it was very nice. She stared at her face and turned it one way, then the other. Her best feature—bony and pretty. High cheekbones. You should go to Paris with that face, her uncles had teased her. You would knock them out up there. But Hoa was not fooled by such talk. Her feet planted in paddy muck by the time she was nine years old.

She adjusted the bra until it did not pinch. She slipped her one nice blouse—bright purple—over her head and stepped into black trousers and gave herself another look. Her feet, bare, were her ugliest feature. Even the GIs noticed. Paddy feet—splayed from working ten-hour days, barefoot. She pulled on pink-and-white-striped socks to hide them, then strapped on sandals.

Hoa went to the window, cranked the louvers, and looked at the canal. It was ancient, wide, waist-deep with the overflow of Mekong water. On the far side it was lined with dark trees and bushes, and the huts of fishermen. On the near side, below, were the concrete docks of the fish market. Women in conical hats squatted behind tin tubs, calling prices to fishermen poling sampans along the dock-side. The prices were low, ridiculous, people weren't buy-ing anymore. The afternoon smelled of musty canal and fish; Hoa loved that. It reminded her of how far she had come already. While her uncles were talking foolishly of Paris, Hoa had worked out her plans.

She was determined. Even now, when she could finally afford to have her laundry done, she got up in the dark-ness, an hour before she had to be at the major's trailer, and at dawn went to the dock and scrubbed her work clothes with harsh brown soap and river water. She would watch the sampans working in pairs out on the river, the fishermen spreading their nets and then drawing them into a circle. Sunrise was the best part of her day and the rest was hard: cook and clean for the major until lunch-time; come home, nap; get up, open the bar, hope some soldiers would drive by and stop in. Still, life was much better here in town. Hoa's plan had been to work in the bar awhile, giving money to her mother, of course, but skimming a piaster here and there, saving for a tub, a town license, and a bribe so she could be a fishmonger too. That was her main plan—to make a nice life here, not far from where she grew up, yet spared the fate of the rice paddies. Which was a lifetime of landlords, cold monsoon rains, wicked sun, backaches at replanting time, threats and questions from soldiers, stray mortar rounds, tripwires, snakes, leeches, ringworm, dark wrinkly skin that could make a girl of twenty look forty-five. Better here. She watched the dock clerk, under the shade of a tin roof, sing

a coaxing auctioneer's song. But the fishmongers called
the lowest prices Hoa had ever heard.

She had the place to herself now but stayed in her old
room. Plain and nearly bare, it had walls of beige cinder-
block, a floor of tiny tiles, a mattress on a wooden bed, a
wide shallow bowl with pitcher for French bathing, and
one white towel. A small trunk held private things: lip-
stick and bobby pins, tooth powder and a purse; a picture
of her father, a tiny bronze Buddha, French fashion magazines, a yellowed, laminated postcard of San Francisco, a
few incense sticks, a gold ring that had been her mother's.
She often practiced rolling it all up in a bundle.

She walked to the doorway, gave a backward glance for
neatness, pushed aside the curtain, and walked down the
hallway. There was something missing—the heavy, acid
smell of GI sweat, the noise of loud deep voices. In the
dark, tiny barroom Hoa felt for the window bolt, threw it,
then drew back the heavy wooden shutter. Ba the bar-
mother had put the shutters in years ago, after QCs had
come through town, a jeepful of them, drunk, throwing
hand grenades.

Out on the street the thin procession of road people—
the timid, the old, the slow—was still going north. A
young woman here, a grandmother and a child there,
three old men far down the road—peasants all of them,
their skin colored and cracked like summer mud. They
limped and shuffled past, headed for Saigon, carrying suitcases, cardboard boxes, bundles, trussed chickens, little
stoves, sacks of rice, babies, small pieces of furniture. Hoa
crossed the room and opened the other window, then
lifted the piece of two-by-four that barred the door. She
opened the door a crack, stuck her hand around the front,
and hung out a faded cardboard sign that said CHAO BAR
AND GRILL, OPEN FOR BUSINESS AND PLEASURE. Bill had made
that sign years ago.

Hoa yawned and sat on a barstool and wished that Ba
the bar-mother had left her the hotplate, for a cup of tea.

But Ba had sold almost everything before she disappeared:
the liquor, the ceiling fans, the red Coca-Cola cooler. All
she had left Hoa was an old radio, brown wood and
shaped like a half-moon. Sometimes Hoa thought she
ought go north, join her real mother, wherever she was in
Saigon, before it got so crowded up there that all the jobs
were taken.

Ba had been forced to close the bar because the GIs
were the best customers, and nearly all of them had gone
north—or, if you could believe the rumors, had gone
home. Ba had given the other girls bus fare, canned food
and rice, and the names of bar-mothers in Saigon—the
best place to be if rumors of a big collapse were true. But
it was hard to know the truth. Even the radio stations lied!
And rumors of a collapse had been going around for all of
Hoa's life.

Hoa refused to go with those girls. Bill had just come
back and it was the surprise of her life. She had argued
and argued and finally Ba had given up; and suddenly the
old woman was gone. She did not go north with the girls.
She was never seen again in town. Someone said she had
gone home to Sa Dec and set up a stand to give tarot
readings, but Hoa took the little bus ride to Sa Dec one
day and found it was not true. Whatever had happened to
Ba was a mystery.

Hoa wondered about her gamble in staying behind. She
played with her hair. She would give her GI—who sometimes, after drinking bourbons, said sweet things to her—
she would give him one week to make up his mind and say
the right words. Sweet-talking was not enough! But even
if he said the right words, the paperwork would take six
months. Because the Big People frowned when their
soldiers took local girls to the U.S. As if Vietnamese girls
weren't good enough. Six months! It was a mean trick by
the American army. A GI was only here for one year, and
by the time he could get to know a decent girl, it would be
too late.

Six months! Surely even the Saigon government could hold back the rebels for six more months. And there was no reason for Bill not to marry her. He had no wife in America—or so he said, they could be such liars these soldiers—but somehow she believed him. He looked as if he had no wife—he seldom even combed his hair! He could certainly afford a wife. And she was decent, with a pretty face, and from a good healthy family. He had a week. Where was he?

She needed to know the time, and walked around the bar to turn on the radio. It could only pull in the strongest station, GI music from Saigon. Saxophone and guitars, with a heavy steady drumbeat. Perhaps Hoa could get used to the harshness of this music if she moved to California; it could be very nice for dancing—even now she was tapping her feet. She looked absently out the window at the Saigon-bound stragglers, a young mother with a baby held at her breast, dragging behind her a rusty wire cart with a burlap bag of rice in it, and bundles tied with kerchiefs, and wilted bunches of watercress. Holding on to the cart was a tiny girl in only underpants and white shoes. The song ended with a high note from the saxophone, and a man's voice, smooth as syrup, said:

Yeah, how about that, those are the Eagles just for you on Armed Forces Radio Saigon. The weather? Oh, it's nice out there if you like it hot. The time? Hey, we're about an hour from sundown.

Hoa sat up startled on the mattress, drew in a breath, brought up the sheet so it covered her to the neck. She put one hand on Bill's bare shoulder. He twitched in his sleep. What was left of daylight came slanting through the louver windows, made a pattern of dark bars and bright stripes across her and Bill. She pushed on his shoulder. He grunted.

QCs—the thought buzzed in her brain, making sweat break out on her soles and palms. She held her breath and listened. For the sound of boots on the floor. For a shuffle of those boots toward the doorway. For a white helmet to appear. For hard brown eyes to see her naked with an American. She pictured herself at the military police station, half dressed, sitting in a plain wooden chair, the QCs rapping their nightsticks, wanting money and confessions.

She found herself in a moment of absolute quiet, with dust motes settling through the bands of light. She became convinced that she had imagined the sound that had awakened her, perhaps bad-dreamed it. Her thin fingers let go of the sheet. She got out of bed, keeping the sheet over

Bill. She crept to the window where her good purple blouse hung from a bamboo hook. She slipped the blouse on, stepped into her underpants, then walked barefoot to the doorway and put her hand at the edge of the curtain. She listened, then parted the curtain the width of an eyeball. No one was out in the bar. Of course she had locked the door. Of course she had remembered.

She took a deep breath, turned around, and looked at Bill. It was amusing to see him this way, his face as peaceful as a boy's, stripes of light across his chest, and the sheet bunched up around his waist and thighs. Such a big man! Hoa had never imagined there could be such big men anywhere—in the French and American magazines they looked normal, but when they got next to you, they nearly shamed you with their size. Bill especially. She remembered when he gave her that first hug, years ago, and she had thought: He's going to squeeze the life out of me.

But no, he was good to her, mostly. Yes, he had left her and broken her heart, and had stayed away for years—but he did come back, after all. And hadn't he asked to come back to Vinh Long so he could be with her? He said so.

No, he had never written her in all those years, but how could he? She couldn't read in English. Besides, from the first day they had met, she had warned herself that he might leave and quickly forget her—after all, they had met in a bar, and she was just a Vietnamese girl.

She walked over to Bill when he started snoring. He got loud after a few drinks, but this was always how it ended —he would talk loud and go to sleep snoring. He never got drunk and hit her, as Vietnamese men had—they were easier for Hoa to figure out. But GIs, what a puzzle! They came to the bar and asked you to sit by them and then pinched you and laughed at you and called you mean names—and then left five hundred piasters as a tip! So generous with their things, so stingy with their hearts— what kind of nation was America, where they raised such a crop?

She put her hand on his cheek, moved his head to stop the snoring. The QCs might hear it out on the street, it was that loud. Back when all the bar girls were here, they used to give private nicknames to the GIs, and Bill they'd named Elephant Voice. Hoa recalled the day she knew she must be in love with him: a payday afternoon, the bar crowded with GIs, and the girls giggled when Bill walked in. They called to Hoa: Here comes your Elephant Voice. They laughed, to know that Bill could not understand them. But that day Hoa did not laugh with them. She found herself thinking: He is very big and strong.

He was coming awake. He reached out both arms for her. *"Men oy,"* he said, and she let herself be drawn into his massive warmth. His breath sour with beer; his face rough with stubble. He mumbled something.

"Gi do?" she said.

He mumbled something that ended with "Sergeant Nuong?"

"He is not here yet," she said. And wriggled out of his arms. "I would like to talk about things."

"What things?" He looked half asleep. Good time for a surprise.

She took a breath, then blurted: "I would like you to marry me . . . and bring me to California."

He closed his eyes and let out a breath, very slowly.

"What is your answer, please?" she asked.

"Hoa," he said, and took a deep breath before he opened his eyes.

"Yes?"

"You don't understand my army. It's not like the Arvin. The American army is all over the world. They could send me to Germany one day and Antarctica the next, and some of those places you couldn't come along. Then where would you be? A foreigner, all alone."

"I would wait for you in San Francisco, California."

"You've never been to California. You have no idea what it's like. You'd be hopelessly lost there."

Hoa sat up. She kept the sheet to her chest with one hand, scolded him with the other. "Sergeant Nuong has been to California. He lived there two years." She held up two fingers as evidence. "Two years! And he never got lost. He told me about beautiful houses and big cars and buildings taller than Saigon."

"Hoa, I can't afford a beautiful house and a big car."

"I would just like to see them."

Bill sighed. "Did Sergeant Nuong tell you about traffic jams? Trailer courts? Smog? Mortgage payments?"

"He told me about stores just like the PX, only bigger, and movie theaters on every block. You cannot lie to me, Bill. I have seen the pictures."

"Hoa," Bill said, and dropped back into bed, closed his eyes, swallowed, then opened his eyes again. "This war isn't going to last forever. When it's over, there'll be a big boom—my country will be giving away money. I can see it in my mind, Hoa. Oil rigs, new factories, new roads. How can I make you understand? If we stay here, we'll have the life of Riley."

"What is a Riley?"

"Let me put it this way," he said, and sat up against the wall. "I know you don't believe me, but in America, we would be poor. We'd end up in a trailer court. That's how I grew up, and I'm not going back to it."

Hoa was puzzled; she looked at him to see if he was trying to trick her; she saw no lying shift to his eyes. "The major lives in a trailer," she said. "And he is the leader, and makes the most money."

Bill breathed out hard, angry. "You don't know what you've got here. I'm not giving it up for a goddamn trailer park."

"These trailers, do they have walls and a roof?"

"Certainly."

"Will we have enough to eat?"

"Of course."

"If I have a baby, will there be a doctor?"

"Yes, an army doctor."

"Then I will be happy in your trailer park."

"You could have the same things right here."

She shook her head. "When the last GI goes home," she said, and drew her finger across her throat, "the VC will crackadau everyone."

"Never happen," Bill said. "There'll be GIs here for fifty years. Have you ever heard of Korea?" He reached out of the bed, to the floor, to get his cigarettes. "Here we could be rich! I know sergeants who retired to Korea, and they're all living great."

Hoa pushed away from him, got off the bed, and stood up. "Do you like me, Bill? Tell the truth, damn you. Why won't you marry me?"

He lit his cigarette and his hands fluttered. It took him three flicks of his lighter to get a fire going. He said: "Just give me time to think it over."

Sergeant Tranh Huu Nuong tried the front door, rattled it, waited, heard nothing, then decided to walk around. He went along the main street, past the moldy apartment building where the Hello and Goodbye was a storefront tenant. Turned down an alley that smelled of fish and sewage, then walked out of the shadows and into fading sunlight at the fish dock. Which was empty except for sampans tied to concrete posts. The fishermen were at home, perhaps drinking tea or beer; the fishwomen were out on the main street, folding their umbrellas, scrubbing their tubs, gossiping.

He counted windows as he walked the dock, and at eight he stood on his toes for a look in. Yes. Lemmen and Hoa were in bed, neither of them moving. Lemmen was bare-chested and Hoa had a purple blouse on. Hoa appeared to be sleeping—or perhaps pouting, her back turned to Lemmen, her face lost in a tubular pillow.

Nuong made a noise like a dove: "Hoo!"

Hoa looked up; one hand went to her throat, then her eyes locked onto Nuong's and she said, "Oi!" and got out from under the sheet. She came to the back door and opened it. She was in her underpants, but completely unashamed. She is not a village girl anymore, Nuong reminded himself, but a city woman—corrupt as they all were. *"Chao co,"* he said to her, and stepped in. Then he looked toward Lemmen. "I am sorry to be so late," he said.

Lemmen reached to the floor for his fatigue pants, brought them under the sheet, arched his back as he zipped them up, then rolled out of bed and onto his feet. "I'll buy you that beer," he said. "Let's celebrate." He shuffled, yawning and barefoot, to embrace Hoa—who, her face puffy and pouty, did not respond. When Lemmen released her, she simply drew on her black trousers and went through the curtain and into the barroom.

In there it was much darker, and Nuong, whose vision had always been poor, had to grope for the bar. He would have liked better light, but both windows were shuttered and it was too close to nighttime to risk opening them. Hoa went behind the bar, where she spent a moment looking at herself in the dim reflection of the mirror. It is not her fault, Nuong told himself, working in the bars makes women vain.

He sat on the stool next to Lemmen at a tiny, Formica-top bar. "Have you got any Monkeys left?" Lemmen asked Hoa. She bent to a galvanized bucket and brought up a brown bottle. "Give it to Sergeant Nuong," he said. "What else is down there?"

"Elephant and Budweiser," Hoa said.

"Anything but Budweiser," Lemmen said. "Haven't you got a 'Thirty-three'?"

She shook her head.

He looked at Nuong. "Tomorrow's my thirty-third. That would have been funny, to have a 'Thirty-three' on your thirty-third."

It took Nuong a moment to realize that Lemmen was talking about his birthday. "Congratulations, Sergeant," Nuong said. This was what they said in America, for some

curious reason. As if the birthday person were responsible
for the luck of living that long.

Hoa got Lemmen an Elephant; as she bent to get it,
Nuong thought he saw a smile pass her lips and didn't
know why. These women! There was no understanding
them. She was angry with Lemmen, though, Nuong could
tell by the way she ripped the cap off with the bottle
opener, the way she placed the Monkey and a glass nicely
before Nuong on a coaster, and shoved the Elephant toward Lemmen without looking at him.

"Ice, *men oy*?" Lemmen asked.

Hoa made a quick, single shake of her head. "No ice."

So the iceman, too, has gone north, Nuong said to himself. He stopped himself from thinking any more about it;
what good would thinking do? He held up the beer bottle
to the cracks of sunlight coming through the shutters. He
looked for floating things: Monkey was a local beer, and
they did not always filter it right, sometimes leaving flies
or bits of straw floating in the neck. Which at one time did
not bother Nuong, but now he was traveled—California,
Hawaii, Singapore—and it seemed that even in a simple
thing like brewing beer, his people were hopelessly behind. He poured beer into the glass; two tiny flies floated
in the bubbles. Why didn't Lemmen ever buy him a
Budweiser? He put down the bottle.

"I have come late," Nuong said, "because I was stopped
by Major Hopkins. He wants to speak to us at breakfast. It
will be five-thirty."

Lemmen finished his beer in one tremendous swallow.
He looked at Hoa, patted the barstool next to him. She
would not come around, and after a moment's staring,
Lemmen turned to Nuong and said: "What's it about? You
probably already know."

"I do not," Nuong said.

Lemmen shook his head. "The old man's senile," he
said.

"He is not old enough for that," Nuong said.

"Then he's crazy," Lemmen said.

"He may be old enough for that," Nuong said,

Lemmen laughed. When he laughed, his belly shook under his shirt and he looked like a big, dark bear. Nuong had not been surprised to find out that his ancestors were Russians.

"I know I am worried, Sergeant Lemmen," Nuong said. He waited for the smile to disappear from Lemmen's face. "I am serious," Nuong said, and waited again. Finally, Lemmen looked receptive; he took out a Lucky and lit it with his lighter, blew a cloud of smoke over Nuong's head.

"Any time the commander wants to talk," Nuong said, "it can only be bad."

Lemmen seemed to consider that for a moment. He puffed on his cigarette. "He's dinky-dau," Lemmen said, and made his index finger circle his ear. "He's stuck down here with no troops, no other officers, I'm his only staff, you're his only connection to the Arvins—and now, this Operation Scarecrow thing . . ." Lemmen stopped and looked around at the doors and windows. Perhaps he realized he had talked too loud.

"Don't worry," said Hoa. "Everyone knows it."

"Knows what?" Lemmen said.

"Delta Town," she said. *"Fini."* She lit a cracked, burnt-down cabaret candle and put it on the bar. The reflected flame was orange on her face. "All day the fishwomen have whispered."

Lemmen sputtered. "Everybody in town knows?"

"Of course," Hoa said.

Nuong looked at Hoa, then at Lemmen. For all the fancy things the Americans had—satellites that took photos from space, telescopes that turned night into day, electric beams that sensed the slightest movements—nothing was as reliable as Vinh Long's gabby fishmongers. Gossip worked so well because the countryside was so backward. No electricity and no refrigerators meant that housewives had to come to market every day. They came in from the villages knowing where the VC had eaten, slept, collected taxes the night before. They exchanged that news for whatever the fishmongers knew about the GIs—information picked up from the townsfolk who worked on base. Even now, Delta Town employed a few local people—Hoa, for one. At its peak the base had employed hundreds of women—housekeepers, maids, and kitchen workers, plus a few old men to clean the outhouses. That was a clue to their weakness, these Americans, Nuong thought. What other army had maids cleaning up after its privates? In what other war did the fishmongers know more than the generals?

"Everybody in town knows!" Lemmen said. "Great. In an hour, the NVA will know. By midnight, they'll be strolling right through the wire."

"No way," said Hoa. And, using Lemmen's beat-up lighter, she lit a second candle, and put it in front of Nuong. "I will hear first," she said, "when the fishwomen whisper."

Command
Performance

"Now look here, Sergeants, I'll lay the whole thing out for you," Major Hopkins said. He spoke and at the same time chewed on bites of toast or forkfuls of scrambled eggs. He had a map spread on the dining table. It showed hundreds of small, plantlike things indicating swamp, and a jagged red border along one side. When the major pointed with his fork, bits of egg fell on the border. "This," the major said, "is Cambodia. Whole regiment of NVA camped out there, waiting for the big one." He tapped his fork on the green splotch that was Saigon. He looked at Lemmen, he looked at Nuong. Nuong felt it would be helpful to nod his head, so he did it.

"Now that's where Operation Scarecrow comes in," the major said. "This was a brainstorm they had up in Saigon, and I want you to know I had no damn say in it." He looked only at Nuong this time. Nuong nodded again.

"Now look here at these little circles," the major said. "These are Arvin posts, strung between Saigon and Cambodia. They've every one of 'em got numbers. Number Twelve is the littlest one, up here near Cambodia, and

Number One is the big one, right outside Saigon. What they've done is taken some local Arvin units and put them out in these posts . . ."

Nuong knew that much, just from the griping it had caused around town. He found himself paying little attention to the conversation—for a moment he watched Hoa, who was in the kitchen scraping papayas. Bone-skinny, her hair pinned up for the day's heat, she worked a big wooden spoon into the heart of the fruit, dug out globs of black seeds. For the whole breakfast she had kept her back partly turned on Lemmen. An excellent strategy, Nuong thought, to keep their secret from the major. Or else she was very angry at Bill.

"So when the NVA comes marching for the capital, they're in for a rude surprise," the major said. "They'll run into one fortified post after another, each one bigger than the last. When they bog down, they'll be tempted to go for an easy target—Vinh Long." He tapped the map and looked at them both.

"There's all that rice in town—they'll be tempted by that, and of course our base is chock-full of weapons and ammo—we're going to leave a few skeletons of helicopters to tempt them. So, there you got it. You now know everything I do." The major spread his arms and sat back, relaxed, and looked toward the kitchen. He was sometimes a crude man, Nuong thought, but he ate very well—tomato juice, a steak coated with batter and deep-fried, fresh scrambled eggs, then papaya with ice cream. The major ate that dessert after every meal. He said it helped with his digestion.

"Sweetheart," the major said. "Could we get the dessert now?" It must have hurt Lemmen to hear her called sweetheart, Nuong thought. Even though it was only Major Hopkins, who got nothing from Hoa but contempt—disguised as obedience. Sweetheart! As though she were a Saigon whore. Hoa put a dish of papaya and ice cream in front of Major Hopkins, then Lemmen, then Nuong. He noticed that she had learned to serve in rank order. She made a small smile at the major, and seemed not to notice Lemmen.

"You can go home, darling," Major Hopkins said. "As soon as you've done the dishes."

Hoa scraped the steak-and-egg scraps, piled up the plates, took them into the kitchen.

"They're all so damn ambitious," Major Hopkins said in a confidential tone. "She's got a second job, you know."

"Oh," said Lemmen.

"I don't know what it is, she won't tell me," the major said. He leaned in toward Lemmen and lowered his voice. "Probably an agent for Charlie," he said. "Tells 'em what I eat for breakfast and how often I shit my pants." He laughed and looked at Nuong. "By God, what are you going to do?"

For a moment no one said anything. No one could eat dessert until the major started, and finally he did. He swallowed a spoonful of ice cream and Lemmen took advantage of the moment.

"Sir," Lemmen said, "Operation Scarecrow is not going to fool the NVA. It's all over town, sir, that we're more or less abandoning the base."

"We want them to know that, Lemmen," the major said. "We want them to think this is an easy target." He paused; a change came over his face. Usually the major looked satisfied and relaxed, but now his face got tight, his eyes moved rapidly; he shook his head. "Well, anyway . . . I didn't dream this thing up, Lemmen—do you think I'd order my own airfield abandoned? I'm taking orders from the colonel, the colonel's taking orders from the general, the general—nobody knows where these things actually start, Sergeant. But I can tell you this: All bets are down now. Wheel's spinning, if you know what I mean."

Those words gave Nuong a tingle of fear starting in his crotch and going up his back. He tried to keep his face impassive. Very gently, he put down his spoon; his appetite for dessert had vanished. He had begun to suspect, weeks ago, what was becoming obvious: If the NVA invaded, Vinh Long and Delta Town Airfield would be sacrificed to save the bigger cities—Can Tho, My Tho, and especially Saigon.

"There's one more thing," the major said, and wagged his spoon at them. "The whole operation depends on how those boys in Post Twelve fight when the NVA comes at them. If they break and run, why . . ." He paused to swallow. He licked the heavy silver spoon clean of melting ice cream. "That's why I'm sending you boys out there."

Nuong felt his skin pucker like chicken flesh. The major paused; he looked at Lemmen, as if waiting for some protest. "No," the major said, "I'm not bucking for light colonel, if that's what you're thinking, Sergeant Lemmen."

"Wasn't thinking that, sir," Lemmen said.

"What were you thinking?" the major asked.

"Well, sir—" Lemmen said.

"Don't think!" the major said, and held his spoon like an exclamation point. "It's the enemy of a great soldier. Don't think. Do! Accomplish! That's a soldier for you."

Lemmen glanced at Nuong. A look that Nuong interpreted as saying: See, I told you he was crazy. Lemmen sipped from his water glass, cleared his throat.

"I know what you're thinking," the major said. "But this won't be combat, Sergeant, because you . . . are not a combat soldier. Is that clear? You . . . are strictly an advisor."

Lemmen breathed out long and hard.

"Do I hear a 'yes sir'?" the major said.

"I suppose so, sir," Lemmen said.

"Good," the major said. "You'll bring 'em two of our old mortars, and give them some good old American training. We'll give 'em enough pop-flares to light up the whole Delta, and enough claymores to blow away the Russian army. Then we'll take 'em out and make sure they know how to run a decent ambush."

"Ambush?" Lemmen said. "Wouldn't that be a violation of the cease-fire?"

"Let me ask you, Sergeant—is the enemy abiding by the cease-fire?"

"No, sir," Lemmen admitted.

"You're damn right they're not. They're raising hell up north right now. But I'll tell you what the thinking is in Saigon. They're thinking that the real push is going to come down here, from Cambodia. Well, let 'em come. Let 'em walk right into our trap." Major Hopkins stood up. He took a few steps one way, and a few the other. "Wait'll the congressman gets an eyeful of the calvary in action."

"Sir," Lemmen broke in. "A congressman's coming here?"

The major seemed totally surprised at the question. "Yes, why, of course he is."

"I didn't know that, sir."

"Of course you didn't know, Sergeant Lemmen. That's why I'm telling you. Now, if it was just any old congressman, why, I wouldn't bother with all this playacting. I'd tell him the lies he wants to hear, give him a two-hundred-mile-an hour ride in a Cobra, and send him home with pee in his pants. But see, this congressman, he's a supporter of ours—I'd like to show him where his money's going."

The major leaned on the table. "They don't call us soldiers anymore, Sergeant. They call us advisors. They call us support personnel. They call us tactical consultants. Next they'll be calling us ballerinas—but I don't care . . ." He reached up and yanked the collar of his uniform; pinned there were tiny crossed swords. "Because in my heart and yours I know what we are—United States Calvary."

Lemmen mumbled something.

"Speak up, Sergeant," the major said.

"It's cavalry, sir. Cavalry, not calvary."

"What the hell's the difference?" the major said, and waved at Lemmen as if to shoo something away. Nuong was puzzled about the difference between *cavalry* and *calvary*. But he didn't get to explore the thought because the major was talking so excitedly.

"Think of it!" the major shouted, standing stiff and tall in back of Lemmen. "It'll be just like the old days. You'll be eating out of tin cans. You won't get to wash for days. You'll be tortured by insects, you'll suffer in unbearable heat, you'll face a ruthless enemy, but you won't give up because you . . . you're calvary!" He seemed to be staring at the ceiling. "I wish to God I could be out there with you."

The major gave them a strange look—as if he had just noticed that they were at the table. He sat down. His face went softer. He put a spoonful of papaya in his mouth and chewed for a moment.

"You'll be out there for two days," the major said. "If it works, you'll give the Arvin a big boost in morale and weaponry, and we'll keep a friend in Congress, and you'll help spring the final trap on the NVA." He smiled. "Maybe," he said, "maybe I'll have a nice surprise for you sergeants once the mission is over. What if I send you up to Little America—how would that be? Sergeant Nuong, I know you've got family up there. And Sergeant Lemmen, I'm going to try my best to get you an early out."

"Well, sir . . ." Lemmen said.

"What can I do for you, Sergeant? Personally, I mean. Staff sergeant? Would you like that?"

"Sir," Lemmen said, "after we get back, maybe you could find me another in-country assignment. Instead of sending me stateside, sir."

"You don't want to go home?" Major Hopkins asked.

"I'd like to stay in the Delta," Lemmen said. "Or no farther north than Saigon, sir."

"Sergeant," the major said, and drew a breath. "How much are you drinking?"

"Reasonable amount, sir."

"Not a quart a day or anything?"

"No, sir."

Major Hopkins made a face of suspicion. "You're not one of those opium smokers, are you?"

Lemmen shook his head.

"Black marketeer?"

"No, sir," Lemmen said.

"It's a woman, then," Major Hopkins said. "Let me tell you, Sergeant, they look mighty good over here, but you'll be sorry once you get 'em home." He leaned in toward Lemmen and said something Nuong couldn't quite hear.

"Sir," Lemmen said, "I was at Fort Carson for the last two years. I hated it, sir. It's cold, it's way up there in the mountains, sir. All we ever did was shine everything, salute everybody. Every morning we went to the motor pool, me and my five men, and filled out forms requesting parts for broken-down personnel carriers. The parts weren't there, but we had to play the game anyway—we'd spend the whole day freezing, polishing a tin can that couldn't start up, or fire a single round. That's no job for a soldier, sir. That's mickey mouse."

"Sergeant," Major Hopkins said. "Now you level with me. Are you CID?"

"No, sir."

"CIA?"

"No, sir."

"Then what are you doing here?"

"I'm your aide, sir.

"I know that, Lemmen."

"Sir, if you don't mind, I'd like that reassignment. I like it here, sir, and now with the war at a stalemate—"

"Stalemate? Why, Charley's getting ready for the big push. If they ever take this country, Lemmen, they'll make the Bolshies look like Camp Fire Girls."

"Sir, won't they have to wait for the U.S. to leave entirely? We're still here, sir, even if it's unofficial. Thousands of us left, isn't that right? And we're going to be here indefinitely. Right, sir?"

The major looked at Lemmen. "Don't ask me, Lemmen, I'm just the man in charge. Hell, if you're crazy enough to stay in this country . . ."

"I am, sir. I've been in places like Carson my whole life. I don't ever want to go back there."

"I'll see what I can do for you," the major said. Then he shook his head slowly, sat back and closed his eyes. At first Nuong could not be sure what was happening; he waited to be dismissed. Then the major's head started nodding.

"Sir?" Lemmen asked.

There was no response.

Nuong had heard stories about Major Hopkins's sleep fits, but had never before witnessed one. He stared at the major's sleeping face for a moment, then got out of his chair, moved noiselessly across the carpet and toward the door. Lemmen stood near the major, as if he couldn't make up his mind what to do. The major made snorts and lip puffs; his head lolled, but he did not open his eyes. Hoa came over, slipped past Lemmen, and pulled the spoon from the major's hand. She took a step back, looked at Lemmen and Nuong, and whispered, *"Didi. Didi mau."*

Lemmen strapped himself in as the whoosh of the rotor blades turned to a roar; he locked the gunner's belt across his belly, tied the string of his boonie hat under his chin, stuck a Lucky Strike in his mouth. He wished he could light the Lucky. He wished a lot of things. As the chopper rose, he snapped the brass snake of ammo into the mud-splattered M-60, swung the gun on its turret, sighted down the muzzle, and wedged his boots into the gun mount to fight the airsick dizziness he knew was coming. His body was on automatic. His mind was busy wondering why, of his own free will, he had chosen to become a soldier.

The helicopter flew nose down over the runway and lifted off, and Lemmen looked over his shoulder, pure habit, as if he still had a squad and it was necessary to count his men. Nuong sat on cases of C rations, his rifle stuck between his legs and pointed down. Under his feet were two mortar tubes, wrapped in canvas; in back of him, piled almost to the ceiling, were cases of mortar ammo, a folded two-man tent with poles, the canvas bag of claymores and flares.

The helicopter noise was overwhelming: squeaking blades, roaring engine. Lemmen closed his eyes, worked the cigarette in his lips, his version of prayer. He didn't believe in any decent sort of God, not any longer, but he found himself pleading with something—the thin air, maybe—that neither he nor Nuong would be the last man killed here.

He felt the helicopter's every bounce, every vibration— the C-ration supper greasy and uneasy in his stomach. Supper had been the second meal that day eaten within sight of Delta Town's runway. Around ten o'clock he and Nuong had gone to the mortar pit, humped the two tubes and all those ammo crates over to the runway—then hurry-up-and-wait had consumed the rest of the day. The helicopter, one of the last in the Delta with an American crew, was busy; to begin with, it was two hours late, and when it did come it had problems and they had to hunt up spare parts; then the pilot had to fly back to Can Tho for a midafternoon priority mission, and when he returned he picked an argument with the major—they'd lifted off six hours late. Now, eyes closed, nerves snappy, patience exhausted, Lemmen, in teeth-jarring flight, imagined that army helicopters didn't fly, not really; they bumped along stupidly on cobblestone roads.

When he opened his eyes and looked back, they were past the Mekong already, maybe five hundred feet up, leaving behind the broad muddy river and, at its edge, Delta Town: a big rectangle with a sandy border, laced with concertina wire, guard towers every hundred yards; inside the base, unused, a metal-plank runway reflected the hazy sun.

Lemmen saw how empty the base was, and that made him feel bad. Delta Town had once been a good home, with a decent PX, a tolerable mess hall, and that fine NCO club. That club had been a real pleasure, offering first-rate drinks for a quarter, other sergeants to commiserate with, a slate-topped pool table, and a jukebox that played songs free. Where else could a man find a life so good and so easy? Lemmen looked down at the tin roof of the club and felt sorry about the day, not so long ago, when the remnants of the 9th Cav pulled out, and the club closed, ruining everything.

He buttoned his shirt against thinner, colder air. He knew he should be scanning the terrain ahead, but couldn't help looking backward: the precise rectangle of the base, the rusty sprawl of the Vietnamese town, and all around, paddies and canals and patches of wild green and the giant snaky Mekong. His eyes focused on the middle of town, a traffic circle, and from there he found the red roof of the Hello and Goodbye. Where he would be right now—if the world were a decent place—half drunk, half asleep, at peace with everybody, Hoa next to him humming a Vietnamese song.

They were up so high now that Lemmen thought he could see Little America. Which was impossible, because it was seventy miles north, but still, a ride in a helicopter did that kind of thing for Lemmen. The altitude gave Lemmen the feeling that he knew what was going on—an unusual thing, when you ranked so low. Officers wouldn't tell you anything until and unless they had to. Your squad is on ambush tonight. Yes, sir. Have your men police the company area. Yes, sir. This is First Sergeant So-and-So, he needs a three-jeep escort down to Soc Trang. Yes, sir. Send three men out to Tower Fourteen on the double. Yes, sir. You were never, never to ask why; it was the forbidden word, and Lemmen was used to that now, after thirteen years in uniform. All you knew for sure were the little things: You'd be up before dawn, you'd make your bed, you'd shave, you'd be given a good breakfast and plenty of coffee. After that, you did what you were told.

Lemmen was always surprised that from this altitude it didn't look like a war zone. It looked peaceful and green

down there. Sort of a wet Illinois, in perpetual summer-
time: fertile and flat, carved into squares, canals straight as
a ruler and running everywhere. He looked over green
paddies stretched out to the horizon and thought: God
Almighty, this is the nicest place I've ever seen.

He hadn't always felt like that; his first frightening
glimpse of it came when he'd been flying for what seemed
like twelve hours from Kyoto, crowded into a TWA jet-
liner with two hundred men and boys. They played cards,
read books, pretended to sleep, stared out the windows.
Lemmen had a window seat, and he stared out, too, trying
to fend off the thought that a lot of guys on that plane
weren't going to make it home, and he just might be one
of them.

It was 1969 and he was twenty-seven years old. Out that
window white clouds streamed over the wing and engines.
The plane drifted down, engines throttled back and quiet.
When he saw a patch of green down there, a jolt of fear
ran through him, but with something else mixed in.
Cloudy seconds went by—minutes—and suddenly it was
green everywhere, green with bright red dirt, craters
blasted in the dirt, smoke rising here and there. The plane
banked, the wings creaked; then it was silent, faces against
windows.

Nobody said anything for a while; then somebody whistled and broke the spell, and guys all over the place started
saying things like *motherfucker* and *Jesus Christ*.

Then there was a whoosh and they landed among familiar army things: helicopters, cargo planes, sandbag bunkers. A stewardess ran down the aisle spraying from a can
of insecticide. The cabin doors opened and the cool air
was sucked out, and in came a hot stink.

Lemmen went down the aluminum stairs, holding the
rails, his legs weak. Walking into that heat was like hitting
a wall; hot waves rose from the runway, and he could
hardly breathe. An old skinny sergeant pointed him toward the shade of a gigantic shed. Hundreds of guys

milled about there, looking for their belongings among a mountain of duffel bags being created by a bulldozer.

They stood around, they sat on their duffel bags, and after a while they were put on a bus that had wire windows. The skinny sergeant, up front, spoke into a microphone, gave instructions about what to do if attacked. Lemmen was not listening, the heat was that bad. The seat was almost too hot to sit in. He was covered with sweat that didn't cool him. Even when the bus got moving, the breeze didn't help—it was like the wind from a hair dryer. Lemmen wiped his face with a bandanna, looked out at the road. Red dirt, and alongside it, grass so tall and thick, it could have hidden an elephant.

The bus turned and suddenly there were people, tiny, skinny people, along the road, on the other side of a flooded ditch. Women squatted and talked, children played and splashed, old men sat in the sun—everyone was dressed in rags. Some lived in the open, with just a cooking pot and maybe a blanket; some lived in cardboard boxes. One old toothless man sat in the biggest box of all, which said WESTINGHOUSE in faded blue. He held a naked baby girl in his lap. When the bus went by, he gave it a stare. It wasn't exactly anger Lemmen saw in those eyes, but some other fierce emotion.

Suddenly a small boy splashed through the ditch and ran toward the bus, and Lemmen realized the kid had something big in his hand. His mind flashed the word *grenade*, the boy let go, and something came up and smashed the wire window just as Lemmen pulled his head back. He got sprayed with a few chips of stone. The boy, already left far back in the road, held up his middle finger.

Some of the GIs cursed, and then someone said loudly: "Welcome to Vee-et-nam." There was a lot of nervous laughter, and before it died the bus was braking for the Little America main gate. As they drove through it, Lemmen tried to cheer himself with the thought that this—

after seven years of stateside mickey mouse—was the real thing.

But for days there was little for new GIs to do; they ate and complained, drank and complained, told morbid jokes and complained, walked around aimlessly, took short, nervous naps, played cards for a lot of money, smoked cigarettes, told homey stories, and waited.

Lemmen began to like it. The tropics agreed with him; the weather was so hot and sticky that, like midwestern winters, enduring it was a matter of pride—the soldiers wore their sweat stains as if they were medals. Little America had the best mess hall outside Washington, D.C., and the NCO club had twenty-five-cent drinks, nickel slot machines, and floor shows with all-girl bands from the Philippines.

At night, rain pounded the barracks roof so hard that the soldiers had to shout their conversations. Around three every morning, sirens sent them scrambling into bunkers, cowering from attacks that never came. By day it was hot, dirty, and exciting. Everywhere were gun jeeps and tanks; helicopters, barbed wire, and sandbags; mounted machine guns; grim, helmeted soldiers; huge artillery pieces. Lemmen was afraid, but there was a thrill in it somewhere. He was finally here; history was being made—and soldiers were making it. He wasn't arranging his footlocker for an inspection at Fort Dix, he wasn't filing manila envelopes in dusty drawers at Fort Ord, he wasn't sitting uselessly, half frozen inside a broken-down tin can at Fort Carson.

The helicopter blades changed pitch, started popping like a machine gun, and made Lemmen realize he was not in the dreamy Little America of years ago, but three thousand feet over the Delta. The chopper banked and he could see how the Mekong split to form an island. It was a gigantic island, so big that Lemmen couldn't see it all; Vinh Long itself, the biggest town on the island, was over the horizon. The island was the key to Operation Scarecrow. If it worked, the NVA would be deflected from Saigon and tricked into going for Vinh Long. Then the Arvins would blow the bridges and trap the NVA between the branches of the Mekong. American Cobras would fill the skies, there would be no choice but surrender.

Lemmen looked over the island; it was dark green, swampy, and misty with its own humidity. He imagined it filled with NVA soldiers, rifles at their feet, hands on their heads.

Minutes later, the helicopter was floating over the flattest, lonesomest, least civilized place Lemmen had ever seen. It was blackwater swamp, spread all the way out to the Seven Sisters, which sat round and purple on the horizon. The highest feature of the swamp was a lone clump of bushes and stunted trees. Lemmen could see no building, no road, no vehicle—no hint of anything human until he looked almost straight down: a mud-brown rectangle with dozens of white dots inside. The helicopter hovered a thousand feet up, the pilot leveling out for a spiral landing —almost a straight drop, in fear of snipers. Lemmen was tapped hard on the shoulder and the crew chief, a giant in a helmet and shield, shouted in his ear, "Hold on."

Lemmen grabbed the struts of his seat, and things started to spin. He shut his eyes and tucked his legs under the seat, then opened his eyes when he remembered he was the gunner. The ship made two full spirals and started nosing up, fanning out, slowing down. Lemmen felt the pressure in his face, his ears; his stomach flip-flopped, the air got hot, they settled into a two-foot hover.

Lemmen turned, and the crew chief, gesturing like a madman, kicked cases of C rations and ammo over the edge. Nuong, M16 slung, one mortar tube in his arms, crouched and sprang out. Finally, Lemmen unstrapped himself, shouldered his pack, slung his carbine, cradled a mortar tube, and all but fell out of the chopper. The crew chief kicked out the last ammo crates, the tent, the two-way radio, the big canvas bag; then he bent and tossed out one of the mortar plates, it weighed a hundred pounds, and he handled it as if it were a discus; then he flung the other one at Lemmen's feet, where it crushed a case of C rations. He gave a thumbs-up to the pilot. The helicopter rose and turned, the prop wash flinging bits of mud into Lemmen's face, the crew chief hanging on to a pole, waving goodbye.

It was just Lemmen and Nuong. Lemmen looked around; the fort was bare, and built of mud. What registered first in his brain were waist-high mud walls, groups of white tents—the biggest one was collapsed—and a ring of curious Vietnamese, keeping a distance. They were men, women, and kids, the men in green uniform. In back of them, a yellow flag with three red stripes hung limp from a dead tree limb.

Lemmen didn't know what to do exactly, so he lit a cigarette; got it out of his waterproof pack and used his beat-up silvery Zippo to turn the end into flame. The helicopter was far away already, noise fading, the sky going deep blue for sunset.

"What do you think?" Lemmen asked. He shook a Lucky up from his pack, held it out to Nuong. Who hesitated before taking it.

Nuong put the cigarette in his lips and made no answer. Lemmen could see his Adam's apple move. He lit the Lucky in Nuong's lips.

"Well," Lemmen said. "Two days. We're here. Might as well try."

"I am not sure what you mean," Nuong said.

Lemmen looked around. "Neither am I," he said. Suddenly he felt foolish and incompetent. "Are you going to introduce us to our hosts?" he asked.

Nuong nodded, sucked in smoke. He turned his head and Lemmen wondered about Nuong's vision. No wonder they'd made him an interpreter, he could hardly see. His eyes looked filmy, and one of them never seemed to focus. Even with his head turned, that bad eye seemed to be watching Lemmen. "Have you noticed?" Nuong said. "We have blown a tent down."

"Tell them we apologize," Lemmen said. "Tell them we'll put it back up for them. I'll do it personally."

"They will still be angry," Nuong said. He threw away his cigarette, not even half finished; it hissed in the mud. "I will go find them out," he said.

Nuong waved to the Arvins and walked toward the commander, a roundish man in a black U.S. Cavalry hat. He'd either stolen it or had bought it off some departing officer's head. Or maybe, Lemmen thought more charitably, it was a gift. The commander—who was the same height as Nuong but twice as wide—began shouting before Nuong got to him. Nuong answered so softly he couldn't be heard, but the commander kept shouting. He pointed at the blown-down tent. Nuong nodded with the suggestion of a bow.

Lemmen turned away, not wanting to see Nuong humiliated. Nothing he could do about it now. He got busy with tactical considerations. Now that they were at ground level, he could see only a hint of the Seven Sisters: a purple haze reflected in far-off clouds. It was enough, though, to give him a sense of direction. Seven Sisters, that's where the NVA would come from. He would set the mortars for that field of fire. By the time they left, the Arvins just might have a chance to deflect the NVA.

But wait a minute, Lemmen told himself. There were, what, fifty soldiers here? Command hadn't given him a number. Command wouldn't tell him anything. Lemmen

turned around to take a quick count. Nuong was still talking to the commander, who had been calmed down; the
two of them had moved beyond the blown-down tent, to
the gathering of men, women, and children. Nuong was
delivering some kind of statement to them. He pointed at
Lemmen, then the sky, then Lemmen, then the sky.

Lemmen thought he would cautiously approach them.
Giving Nuong, of course, time to complete his introduc-
tion. He thought he would nod and smile and ask Nuong
to explain that he had brought good things—weapons and
food. He was walking toward them when a boy broke and
ran toward him. A boy maybe ten years old, skinny and
barefoot, wearing shorts and a torn muddy white shirt. He
stopped just short of Lemmen and stared.

Lemmen stepped back; he had seen many boys like this:
dirty, dressed in muddy clothes, hair long and unwashed.
Lemmen slung his carbine over his shoulder, squatted,
and looked the boy in the eyes.

"What do you want, little man?" Lemmen said.

The boy looked at Lemmen, eyes big and brown. Teeth
huge and pure white. Skin the color of swamp mud. His
lips quivered. Maybe he was nervous and trying to smile.

"You want gum?" Lemmen said. He had never met a
Vietnamese boy who did not understand certain English
words.

The boy didn't say anything, but tapped Lemmen's left
shirt pocket. Which was where Lemmen had his red radio,
buttoned in tight. For a moment he was puzzled, then he
got it. He opened the flap of his other pocket. "You mean
these," Lemmen said. "Cigarette." He showed the boy his
Luckies, the red circle showing through the yellow plastic
pack. "I guess one won't hurt you."

He opened the pack and got out a Lucky. Held it out
but the boy wouldn't reach for it. "What's the matter?"
Lemmen asked. "Why don't you tell me. Why so quiet?"

The boy shook his head, turned his lips down in disgust,
and said: "Say-lem." He held out a muddy palm.

The first bit of orange sun slipped beneath the flat horizon and Lemmen, on one knee, binoculars hanging from his neck, stared into a scope mounted on the mortar tube. Fifty feet away, Sergeant Nuong speared a red-and-white aiming stake into the mud. Lemmen tapped his boonie hat on the left side. Nuong tilted the stake.

Lemmen tapped his hat again. Then he stood up, backed away from the tube, and with both hands waved for Nuong to come in. He put a hand on the aching small of his back. Just today turned thirty-three, and already the creak of age. He wiped his hands, slimy with gun grease, down the thighs of his trousers.

He opened one of the wooden crates they had stacked in a semicircle around the mortar. "What's on the menu tonight?" he said. "H.E. ? A little illume?" In the crate, black cardboard cylinders were wedged into V-slots and surrounded by greasy brown paper. Lemmen lifted one cylinder and pulled a string tab—it opened like a pack of cigarettes. He took out a mortar round, a miniature bomb with a conical tip of solid brass, an olive-drab body, aluminum fins surrounded by small yellow sacks. "Good old H.E.," Lemmen said—he was talking to himself; Nuong was slow coming in. "We'll put these on the right. We'll keep the illumes on the left. Let's arm for . . . six H.E. and three illume."

Lemmen looked over his shoulder to see where Sergeant Nuong had gone: he was talking to a group of Vietnamese, all uniformed men, halfway across the compound.

"Okay," Lemmen said, "I'll do it myself." Putting it that way made him feel lonesome. "Fire mission," he shouted. Saying those words jazzed him. This is what he'd been trained for—Eleven Charley, mortarman. "Deflection twenty-one hundred mils," he shouted, "elevation two feet." With no assistant gunner to help him, he had to kneel in front of the chained legs of the mortar, pick them up, set them down; then he moved in a squat toward the scope, looked in. The cross hairs were nearly centered on the stakes. Good enough for a practice round.

He stood and put the binoculars to his eyes. Kept talking to himself, softly. "See that little clump of bushes out there? We want to come down right smack in the middle of it." He brought down the binoculars and turned around. "Okay," he said to himself.

"Okay," said Nuong, behind him.

"Crept up on me," Lemmen said, and smiled. "Do you want to go over what we're going to show these guys tomorrow?"

Nuong shrugged. "I am sure we must."

Lemmen took a step toward the gun. "Maybe you can think about how we're going to explain it. Let's run it through." He made a noise in his throat, clearing the way for a more aggressive and commanding tone. "One round Hotel Echo. Make sure it's a Hotel Echo you've got in your hand. It should be a green one. Put the round in the mouth of the tube, fins first, like so." Lemmen held his hands in a circle, pretending to hold a round inside the mouth of the gun. "Turn your face away. Wait for the crew leader to say 'fire in the hole.' Then let the round drop, bringing your hands down along the tube like this . . ." He pretended to let the round go, then dropped to one knee, sliding his hands along the tube. "That way, you'll never lose a finger."

He pushed himself up. Looked at Sergeant Nuong. "What do you think?"

"It is very understandable," Nuong said.

"Good," Lemmen said. "I forgot to mention the charge bags." He resumed his deeper voice. "Charge bags are these yellow things," he said, holding up a mortar round. "The more you leave on, the farther the round goes. If you leave too many on, it'll go over their heads. Too few and you'll be ducking it yourself. So pay attention to the charge bags! If the crew leader says charge three, the gunner will strip off all but three bags. Ready?" He looked at Nuong. "Pretend you're the crew leader. Say 'charge three.' "

"Charge three."

Lemmen ripped off yellow bags; they fell at his feet, and he put the round in the mouth of the tube. Fins pinged against gunmetal.

"Say 'fire in the hole,' " Lemmen said.

"Fire in the hole."

Lemmen let go, brought his hands down the tube, dropped to one knee. The round slid, metal sounding on metal, it seemed to take a long time to fall—then came an explosion so loud and close that Lemmen didn't hear so much as feel it; concussion, then a painful ringing in his ears. He stood up. The air smelled of explosive. He raised his binoculars and waited, his eyes fixed on the clump of bushes. After what seemed like five minutes, there was a white flash in front of the bushes, then a puff of gray smoke, a crack and a boom. Lemmen grinned and whistled. "Pretty close," he said, and turned, expecting to see a grin on Nuong's face.

There was only a worried look; Nuong's thin face was tight, his good eye watery.

"Not bad shooting for a two-man crew," Lemmen said, hoping that Nuong's worries had nothing to do with him. "One shot and we're zeroed in." Nuong's face twitched. Lemmen couldn't avoid it any longer. "What's the matter?"

"I have been thinking," Nuong said. "If this plan does not work, Sergeant . . ." He stooped to the ground. Drew a line in the dirt. Stood up. "I will have to cross the line."

"What are you talking about?"

"This line," Nuong said, and pointed down.

Lemmen could not figure it out.

"This line I have not crossed yet. Please give me a cigarette."

Lemmen reached for two Luckies, gave him one. It was getting dark fast; the flame of Lemmen's lighter cast a glow on Nuong's cheek. Nuong sucked deep, held the cigarette out and looked at it. "It tastes good indeed," Nuong said.

Lemmen nodded and blew out smoke.

"I have been trying in my own way, Sergeant," Nuong said. "Do you remember yesterday, when you passed by the tower? It was not for discipline that I whipped that young boy. I was hoping to make him run away."

"Why?"

"There is no use defending Vinh Long, is there? To be killed there would be to lose your life to a trick. So I gently stepped on the line. Enough have been killed already. So I have stepped on that line, but never over it."

He drew on his cigarette. "But out here, I am no longer sure. I think there is a chance, Sergeant, to keep the NVA out of Saigon. It is a small chance but I suppose it is the only one we have." He drew on his cigarette. "But If we succeed, we will be luring the NVA toward Vinh Long."

"True," Lemmen said. "But that's part of the plan."

"My family is in Saigon," Nuong said. "My friends are in Vinh Long."

"I don't think the NVA will ever get to Vinh Long," Lemmen said.

"You still have faith in things," Nuong said. "This is something I wish I had." An emotion passed Nuong's filmy eyes; he threw his cigarette away. "In the meantime, Sergeant, we have problems," he said, and stepped back from the line he had drawn in the dirt, walked a circle around it. "The Dai-ui does not want us here. He did not ask for us to come."

"We brought him claymores," Lemmen said. "We brought him mortars." He patted the tube, which rang like a bell. It was warm, an old friend. "This will help him hold off Charley."

"I told him that," Nuong said. "But he doesn't believe. The Dai-ui says if the NVA come, he will need a Cobra strike."

Lemmen walked around the outside of the ammo crates and once again faced Nuong. "Doesn't he understand the plan? The Cobras aren't going to fly until his soldiers help trap the NVA on the island."

"He understands," Nuong said, "that you cannot fire mortars when helicopters are flying, and so he knows what it means that we have brought mortars. You see, when Colonel Tho put the Dai-ui out here he promised Cobras."

Lemmen thought for a moment. "Then Colonel Tho lied."

"It is not unusual," Nuong said. "Nobody cares to tell them the truth." He looked over his shoulder toward the white tents. "Some of us are lucky," he said.

"What do you mean by that?"

"Some of us will leave."

The radio was playing rock music, and inside the tent, it sounded tinny, and muted for the night. The station played the only American music Lemmen could pull in—although he couldn't figure out what station it was. AFVN was all static, and the Can Tho station didn't broadcast at night.

Anyway, he wasn't paying much attention—rock 'n' roll was not his music, and it all sounded alike to his ears. Except for the real oldies, from back in the fifties, when it was still half country. A guy could go months without hearing a decent Hank Williams, so Lemmen had long since surrendered to hoping for an oldie—comforted, at least, by whatever country twang was left in the voices.

The music drifted toward squealy static and Lemmen picked up the radio, shook it, fingered the dial, tuned the station in again. The radio was a seven-dollar clearance special from the Pacex catalogue, that Sears, Roebuck of the war. Amazing what guys ordered from that catalogue: refrigerators, diamond jewelry, Seiko watches, cameras and lenses, color TVs, air conditioners, and, of course, stereos, stereos, stereos. Back in '69, his squad owned enough electronic stuff that Lemmen had wondered whether he was in a war zone or a stereo zone.

He swatted at a mosquito. Which was one of a squadron dive-bombing his ears. He'd already applied half a bottle of mosquito oil to his face, hands, and neck; but with this breed of mosquitoes, repellent seemed to attract them. He swatted again, killed one on his neck. Felt the blood from it.

It was dark. No sense staying sober, especially on his birthday. He turned and searched his pack for his pint of Grand-dad. Unscrewed the top, brought the bottle to his lips, held the whiskey in his mouth, stinging warm. Took a mouthful of water from his canteen. Was sorry he did that, the water hot, smelly, and full of iodine.

He felt like writing a letter, but had nobody to send it to. Unless you counted his father, and he didn't. He had no woman back in the World—he'd never stayed still long enough. Even in high school he had gone steady with just one girl, for three months, until she stunned him by handing back his school ring. He'd never been able to figure out what he'd done wrong. I'm breaking up with you, Bill, she said—he could still hear her say it—you're looking for the perfect girl, she said, and I'm not her and I don't think you'll ever find her. That girl, Peggy McCoy, got married a year later, and started having babies, and for all Lemmen knew was still living happily in Rock Island.

He counted it up—fifteen years and he'd only been back once, under the worst of circumstances. He had no friends left there, that was for sure. He'd made plenty of friends in the army, but they weren't the letter-writing kind. He couldn't imagine a guy like Worthington, for example, writing a letter, or even reading one. He didn't even know Worthington's address, except that he was in-country— probably he'd have the cushiest job at Little America. Anyway, army friends were the kind that you didn't hear from in eight years and then you met them at Benning or somewhere and you'd go off for a week of whoring and boozing like you were lifelong buddies—and then boom, they were shipped out.

Which left only Hoa, but she couldn't read English. Lucky she could read Vietnamese; she had gone only up to the sixth grade. Still, that was a long way for a girl, and only the brightest got that far. But Lemmen had refused to teach her to read or write English. Why encourage her crazy dreams of America? If they ever got serious as a couple, they were going to stay in the Delta. Period. Certainly not in some sleazy town outside a U.S. Army base. Where did that girl get her idea of the States anyway? What retired sergeants lived in postcard houses in San Francisco? He wished he could take Hoa for a quick, convincing trip through the trailer parks, gas stations, taco stands, and stinking ginmills of a military town like Seaside, California.

He lit a smoke, realizing after he clicked the lighter shut that he was showing the only light; his radio was giving off the only human noise. He wondered about the families not a hundred feet away—trapped inside a tent for an eleven-hour night. What did they do with themselves? Their tents must be buzzing with mosquitoes. How did they sleep? Why hadn't they gotten real tents? Instead of converted parachutes that stood out like ghosts—like targets. It wasn't as if there were no surplus tents at Delta Town.

Even with the radio on, Lemmen couldn't shut out the noise of the swamp. It had started with a chirp at sundown, and grew to a roar. He had never heard that many insects making noise that loud. It was ceaseless. Dangerous, too, Lemmen thought, because Charley could use that noise as cover to sneak up on them.

He felt for his carbine. Lifted it into his lap. Started to feel better. Stubbed his cigarette out and it was utterly dark in the tent. A coward's thought crossed his mind—if Charley snuck in, his dark, low tent was not likely to be attacked. Unless, of course, Charley heard the music. It was only seven-thirty, not a typical time for Charley to attack. Still, Lemmen gave himself a half-hour deadline for radio silence.

Some birthday, he told himself. But he promised himself a real celebration when they got to Little America. He fumbled in the dark and found a can left over from his C-ration dinner. Flicked on his amber-shielded flashlight, took the P-38 opener off his boonie hat, cut into a can of fruitcake. Lit a fresh cigarette and stuck it in the fruitcake like a candle. Groped for his bottle of Grand-dad and took a long chug. Then turned off the flashlight; for a moment the light seemed to linger, and the tent was golden inside before turning pure dark again.

Another rock 'n' roll song. That made it three or four in a row without a commercial. Without a reminder about VD or your obligation to the Red Cross. Decent station. Lemmen tried to enjoy the music. Leaned back on his pack and thought about Hoa.

Which always made him feel warm, between the legs and elsewhere. What was it about that girl? Something. Pure chemistry, as far as he could figure out. Why did he like her so much? She was so skinny, her body all blotchy. But he loved the feel of her and the look of her too: skin and bones, ugly and beautiful at the same time; small, exotic, vulnerable. He closed his eyes and tried to imagine her—he could almost smell her. Command was right, this morning, when he leaned over to Lemmen and said that these women smell like fish. They did! Hoa included. She smelled like fish, like the swamp, like the Mekong—and the memory of her scent was driving Lemmen wild, he wanted to take her long black hair in his hands, run his tongue along her body.

He lost that vision, couldn't get it back. Found himself thinking over what Nuong had said—couldn't block it out of his mind. If he did his job out here, he would be pointing the NVA at the town where Hoa grew up. A town that Lemmen had grown to like. Full of people who had never done him any harm. What if the NVA did get there? He didn't want to think about that. He could make sure Hoa got out, but what about her friends, neighbors, cousins? What about these people out here? Would these mud-fort soldiers last a minute in the face of the NVA? Maybe it would be better if Lemmen didn't do his job. Maybe he, Nuong, the Dai-ui, and all the Arvins should *didi-mau* at the next low tide.

But then they'd all be traitors. Anyway, where would they go? And what would happen then? The NVA would simply walk past this post and attack the next one. What if all the soldiers at all the posts deserted, and the NVA marched into Saigon? The thought made Lemmen go cold. The only way, he told himself, was to follow orders.

"Boys."

That voice on the radio, female and shrill, startled Lemmen, and he knew immediately who it was, without having heard her before. Ho Chi Minnie.

"Boys, boys, boys," she said, "you see with your own eyes the poorness of our small nation. We have so little to offer you. You have so much at home."

There was a long pause; she could have been flipping a page.

"Boys, your longing for home is quite natural. Our soldiers, too, long for their simple homes. Our soldiers, too, have lovers and wives, fathers and mothers waiting anxiously. Does it not seem a shame, boys? The war is over but you are not allowed to leave. Why is this? Your government has let so many go home. Then it denies to all the world that you are here. You see, the war is forgotten already in America."

A pause.

"Our freedom fighters have promised to go home as soon as the last GI does. Then we will all enjoy the blessings of peace."

A subtle change came over her voice, and she said: "My

good boys, my abandoned boys, my homesick boys, this next song is for PFC George Garfield, who is temporarily in Chu Lai but whose real home is Selmer, in the Tennessee of your beautiful country."

Lemmen snapped off the radio. After a moment of seeming silence there was the roar of insects and the chronic mortarman's ringing in his ears. He felt the wooden stock of his carbine. He had a name for it: Sam. He'd traded a good little Sanyo refrigerator for Sam, back in '69 at the Hello and Goodbye. He traded with a sleazy Arvin deserter named Liu who'd been hanging around town, selling everything from heroin to Honda cyclos to Coca-Cola. The trade was too good to pass up. Sam was an M-2 carbine, a sawed-off relic of World War II, and was nothing like the M-16—that rifle was a big disaster. Lemmen could never understand why the army still issued them. Sixteens were temperamental; get a little dirt on them and they would blow up in your face. They needed to be babied, like certain draftees he'd known. But Sam was like an old sergeant—crusty and dependable. Sam didn't look like a space-age weapon, didn't fire a million rounds a minute, but he was made out of real wood and real steel and you could pick him out of the mud and he would fire.

Suddenly Lemmen got goose bumps and brought Sam up out of his lap. "Who's there?" he shouted. Felt his hair stand on end. His scalp like a helmet. No answer.

Slowly, carefully, silently, he moved the rifle safety off. He listened.

Just the insects, just the ringing in his ears. He kept the rifle pointed at the tent flaps.

He sat there sweating, stomach in cramps, skin tight across his face. A minute, two minutes, three minutes— could have been any length of time. He knew he would have to look outside. He moved quietly from sitting to squatting to prone. Did a silent low-crawl to the tent flaps. Rifle up, butt jammed in his armpit, he eased the muzzle through the flaps. Then drew it back, rolled to the side of the tent.

Waited. Heard himself breathing. He stuck the muzzle out, slowly parted the flaps with it.

Moonlight. The half-moon had come up and Lemmen could almost see. Gave him enough confidence that he stuck his head out, and after a long look, hauled himself out of the tent.

Nothing there but a couple of C-ration cases. In a crouch, he went around the back of the tent, his finger loose on the trigger. Nobody back there. Nobody anywhere. He walked all the way around, let out a long breath. Sam sagged in his arms.

"Hey!" A flash of something white. He had the rifle up and then realized it was a kid. He let the rifle down. The kid had stopped, frozen, as if that would make him invisible. He'd been hiding near the C-ration cases.

"*Lai day,*" Lemmen said to the kid. The boy had his hands up; he wore a white shirt that glowed in the dark. Lemmen didn't know how to say "put your hands down." He tucked Sam under one arm as the boy walked up to him. It was the same kid who, a few hours before, had asked him for a Salem.

"Here," Lemmen said. He reached out and put the kid's hands down; they went back up. Lemmen forced them down. "What's your name?"

The kid shook his head.

"Not going to tell me?"

"No *bic.*"

"Name," he said, and pointed to the kid. "You."

"No *bic,*" the kid said.

Lemmen pointed to himself. "Bill."

The kid laughed, and Lemmen wondered what was funny. Then the boy pointed to himself and said: "Van."

"Van," Lemmen said. "Caught you stealing C rations, didn't I. Hungry?" He pointed to his own stomach. The boy nodded yes. Lemmen reached over into the big carton of C's, which was torn halfway open. Give the kid something decent, he thought, and tried to read the labels by moonlight. Ham and limas? No way, he'll grow up to join the VC. Maybe turkey. "Eat?" he said, and showed the kid a box.

"Okay," the boy said. Lemmen searched his top pocket for his P-38. It was in the tent. "Come on," he said to the kid, then took him by the wrist.

He pushed open the flap, crawled to the back of the tent, fumbled for his flashlight, and turned it on. The boy came in and sat opposite him, barefoot, thin legs sticking out of shorts. This boy isn't starving, Lemmen thought, but he's not eating right, either. He opened the box. Worked the opener into a can of turkey. Then ripped open a cellophane bag and handed the boy a plastic spoon. Held the open can of turkey meat under the boy's nose. The boy smelled it, made a face. "Number ten," he said. His lips curled in disgust.

Lemmen opened the cans of cheese and crackers. Demonstrated by dipping a cracker into cheese. The boy just shook his head. "Can't be too hungry, then," Lemmen said. The boy stared at the cellophane pack, and Lemmen threw it to him. He tore through it. "Salem! Salem!" he shouted, and held up the green-and-white pack. A terrific grin on his face, big teeth. He took the Hershey's tropical chocolate bar, the Salems, the matches, the Chiclets, stuffed them all in his shirt pocket. Leaned toward Lemmen and said something in Vietnamese.

"What?" Lemmen said.

The boy pointed.

"Ray-dee-oh," Lemmen said.

"Van," the boy said, and pointed to himself.

"Oh, no, I'm not giving you that," Lemmen said.

The boy reached forward, turned the dial, upped the volume to loud static. Then, looking carefully at Lemmen, he took the radio, sat back, put it in his lap.

Lemmen raised the can of turkey to his own nose. "I'll

eat it if you won't." The boy was entranced by the radio. Lemmen dug out a spoonful of meat. "Delicious," he said. But Van ignored him. Then he got something on the radio.

"Boys," the woman's voice said. She breathed a deep, theatrical sigh. "You are the victims of such a hopeless, hopeless dream of conquest."

"Give me the radio," Lemmen said, and then tried it in pidgin: "Radio, me." When he reached for it, Van sprang up, slipped past the flaps, and was gone.

Sergeant Nuong lit a candle. The blue-yellow flame flickered in front of a picture of his brother Albert. It was a wallet-size photo and Nuong had set it on a small, crude altar in a tent—the same tent that the helicopter had blown over coming in, and that Nuong, working by himself, had resurrected. The altar was a pile of empty U.S. ammo crates and Nuong knelt at it, hands knotted into fists.

The photo was of Albert in death, and the morticians had done their best on the twisted skin just above the right eyebrow. Where a dark, bloodless hole seemed tiny, innocent, hardly capable of causing so much damage and heartbreak. Albert had made it only to twenty-four years old. He had been a bus driver and—everyone's second occupation—a soldier. He had been dragged out of his bus near the Can Tho ferry one afternoon by three teenagers, shot once, and left dead like a run-over dog in the road. He had a wife and baby daughter; there had been no picture of just him anywhere, and now, in his only pose, his eyes were weighted closed, his shoulders draped in the white blouse of death.

It was easy to feel bitter. Deaths such as Albert's were nothing—they were not even reported in the papers, except as numbers: ENEMY AGENTS KILL FIVE DESPITE CEASE-FIRE. So what? Everyone was suffering. Every family in some stage of mourning. On his last visit home he'd heard his parents comforting themselves, saying: Albert died a brave man. Lying words of comfort the priest had put in their heads at the funeral. More likely, Nuong thought—but never told his parents—Albert died begging for life, his teeth chattering and shit in his pants.

Now he was out of it, at least, but Nuong sometimes had trouble remembering him. They had gone to different schools—Albert for French and Tranh for English; their parents had thought they were making good bets for the future. Albert had been a superb soccer forward and a bright but indifferent student—he said he despised the French, but clung to the French name he'd picked up at school. He'd had many girlfriends and was frequently drunk. He had a sly smile. More than once he had slapped his wife over one thing or the other, but she loved him and still dressed white with mourning. That was all that Nuong could seem to remember, not much from almost twenty-five years. He wished—sometimes, against all reason, he prayed—for an hour with Albert, so they could talk about things proper to brothers: jobs and troubles and wives and politics and how they were as children—just an hour for all the things they had foolishly left unsaid.

He reached out and touched his finger to Albert's picture, then stood up. He picked up the candle, tilted it, lit incense sticks on either side of the photo. Passed the candle in homage before the gods, who were set on a top shelf: a framed photo of Victor Hugo as an old man, a wooden image of Sun Yat-sen, a small white-bone Christ on a white-bone crucifix, a sitting brass Buddha.

A mixed-up religion, or so the Big People thought.

They laughed at it. The single all-seeing eye of God, that was what these people worshiped. An eye inside a pyramid, exactly like the one on the back of an American dollar. Jesus, the Buddha, a French poet, an Asian general—they were just the helper gods. It was the one truly Vietnamese religion, and it had an attractive unity, Nuong thought, although he was no believer. But then he didn't believe the Buddhists or his own Catholics either.

He picked up the photo of Albert, brought it up to his good eye, and looked closely. Nuong had been born with a bad eye; nobody had ever thought of trying to fix it. One of the amazing things about America was the health of the people. If something was wrong with someone, it would be fixed. Even ordinary people seemed perfect. In Vietnam, everyone had a defect or disease, that was normal. Nuong scanned the fading image of his brother. Albert had been a stunning exception. He had been strikingly handsome and perfectly healthy. But now mold ate at the edges of the photo, and in a few more humid months, even his death image would rot away. Nuong folded the photo into his wallet, gave a glance at the single eye of God. He suddenly wanted to spit at it. He stepped out of the tent. It was quiet except for the insects, and dark except for the moon.

He lit a cigarette he had gotten from Lemmen. He kept it hidden by his wrist except when he brought it up for a quick puff. He walked the mud path among tents that glowed—not from lights inside, but from their color and the moonlight. White was not a good color for a soldier's tent. But these people had taken what was handed to them —GI parachutes—and put them up on poles.

He sat on an ammo crate between Lemmen's dark tent and the rows of ghostly Arvin tents. He could smell the lingering aroma of a good supper—rice and grilled fish. Nuong had not eaten. He seemed to be growing skinnier by the week. His forearm stuck out of his sleeve, all bone.

He did not like C rations. But he could not eat with the

Arvins either: they smelled too much of doom. Eating with the soldiers was one thing, but the women and children—he could not stomach the thought, the sight, the voices of those living ghosts. He didn't want to know their names. No one in the Arvin high command even imagined that they would survive, Nuong was sure of that. The commanders only hoped that the NVA would tire of battling for post after post, and, after they had overrun this and a few others, take an easy, fatal turn toward Vinh Long.

The Dai-ui must have made a mistake, to have been sent out here. His mistake was probably to be of the wrong religion. No matter what anyone said, the Saigon Catholics were still in charge, and when the commanders mobilized for Operation Scarecrow, they must have deliberately picked Dai-ui Loan's unit for this farthest outpost. In order to make sure the soldiers did not simply run from an attack, Saigon had done its usual trick of sending along the wives and children—with the excuse that family life would improve the soldiers' morale.

They might all be dead in a week, Nuong thought. If they lasted that long! Saigon's only hope was that they would at least fight. After the war, the prosperous in Saigon would call these people martyrs and heros. Even the honest people—intellectuals, historians—would say so. Perhaps one distant day in the capital, an official would glorify them in a lofty speech, dedicate a monument to them and call them patriots. Perhaps he would recite their names.

Nuong stubbed out the cigarette on the side of his boot, careful to save a few puffs for later. Was he any better than the Arvin commanders? He, too, had given in to selfishness, he was working for the success of Operation Scarecrow, so he had sided with the elite in Saigon. But what choice did he have? He sat there thinking of the past and the future and felt suddenly cold.

"Quiet, Sergeant Nuong?"

"Yes," Nuong said. He heard Lemmen sit down in the dark beside him. Nuong was leaning back against a splintery ammo case, claymore clackers at his side, an M-16 in his lap.

"You can go to bed now," Lemmen said.

"I am not quite sleepy," Nuong said. Their voices weren't very loud, but they weren't a whisper either, against the insect noise of the swamp. "I'll stay up awhile."

"Good, keep me company," Lemmen said.

Nuong pushed the clackers toward Lemmen. Not that he could see Lemmen or much of anything else. The moon was a half circle of gray light behind misty clouds; the stars were completely lost. Nuong could see the outline of the mud wall, three feet high and just in front of him; beyond it only shades of darkness. He had long ago stopped looking for things in the dark. Too many times he had been fooled by ghosts, figments, hallucinations, illusions. If he sat alone all night and stared with one eye into the darkness, he would see all the frightening things of his mind; so he had learned simply to listen.

He listened to Lemmen settling in: the scrape of his boots in the dirt, the click of his ammo bandoliers, the plop of his boonie hat hitting the ground, the raspy squeeze of a plastic bottle. Then came a chemical smell.

"Want some bug juice?" Lemmen asked.

"No, thank you," Nuong said.

"Aren't they biting you?"

"They are."

"Take some, then," Lemmen said. The plastic bottle touched Nuong's arm. He did not reach for it. "For me, it is better not to," he said.

Lemmen withdrew the bottle and said, "Okay."

A mosquito buzzed Nuong's ear. He reached up, closed his palm over it, squeezed. Another one landed on the back of his neck; he killed it without making a smacking sound. But Nuong knew that sometime in the night, while on the next guard duty or perhaps while trying to sleep, he would give up and let them bite.

For quite a while, it seemed, no one said anything. The swamp made its noise: a symphony of twirps, cheeps, splashes, croaks, tweets. Nuong had become very good, over the years, at listening to it. A rat and a man's foot were the same size, and made a similar sound in the water, but Nuong could tell the difference. A swamp rat made an innocent, uninhibited splash; a man's foot moved with a sneaky ripple.

He listened. He heard Lemmen unscrew the cap of a bottle, then caught a whiff of bourbon. He heard a gurgle; after a moment the cool bottle was pressed against his bare arm. Without saying anything, he brought the bottle up to his lips for a small sip, then another one, and passed it back into Lemmen's hot and sweaty hand.

"Tomorrow," Lemmen said, "I would like you to do something for me."

Nuong, for a moment, was sorry he had taken the drink.

The GIs always put you in debt this way. They gave you a drink of their excellent whiskey, or a pack of menthol cigarettes, or an 81-millimeter mortar, and wanted something in return.

"That boy Van went away with my radio," Lemmen said, and passed the bottle. Nuong's resentment subsided. For sure, Lemmen was not the worst GI. Most of them would have accused the boy of stealing. Lemmen, at least, understood the value of diplomatic talking.

"It's a cheap radio," Lemmen said. "If the PX was still in business, I'd just buy another one." Nuong took a long sip and put the bottle back into Lemmen's hand. "But I was hoping maybe you could talk to the boy's parents . . ."

"I believe he has no parents," Nuong said. "He looks dirty, like a camp child. He would be in care of the Dai-ui."

There was no talking for a while. Nuong listened to the swamp.

"I won't ask you to bother the Dai-ui," Lemmen said.

"It will not be necessary," Nuong said. "I will take that boy by the arm and he will get your radio. I'm sure he has hidden it by now."

"No, that's all right," Lemmen said, then gurgled a sip from the bottle, passed it to Nuong. "He's an orphan, isn't that what you're telling me? Let him have the radio."

"Don't do that," Nuong said. "It will only teach him to steal," Nuong said. "Besides, it is forbidden in this camp that they should have a radio." He didn't feel like drinking any more. He passed the bottle back to Lemmen.

"It's what?" Lemmen asked.

"It is forbidden that they should have a radio," Nuong said. "They may have military kinds only. Saigon does not want them listening to the other side's propaganda."

"Or hearing the news," Lemmen said.

"You may say that," Nuong said.

"I'll get the radio back myself," Lemmen said.

"I will help you," Nuong said. They didn't talk for a moment; Nuong listened to the insect noise.

"What happens to a boy like that?" Lemmen asked. "Eventually, I mean."

"He will follow the army around until he is old enough," Nuong said.

"To carry a rifle?" Lemmen asked.

"Yes," Nuong said.

Lemmen offered another drink; Nuong refused by gently pushing the bottle away. After a while with no talking Lemmen said: "His parents were killed?"

"Or perhaps they deserted."

There was a splash and Nuong put a hand on Lemmen's shoulder and made a tiny hiss for silence.

For a moment it seemed quiet. Then Nuong heard Lemmen snatch up his carbine, heard insects and frogs and then another splashing noise. Nuong could not make up his mind about it; a few more splashes and he would know. He silently moved his M-16 safety two stops to full automatic.

For what seemed like a long time he listened without hearing a splash. Then came a sucking sound. Then after perhaps a minute, a ripple. There was a pattern, a timing to it, all Nuong needed to know. A tingling fear came from his crotch and spread like numbness through his body. Nuong fought it with reason: This must be a one-man probe. No squad could move in such coordination as to sound like one man. He heard a sucking sound, then a ripple, coming a minute apart. Let him come closer, Nuong thought, let him sweat, let him worry, let him sneak in for the next hour while we listen; we're behind the wall, we have the claymores, and sooner or later we will see a reed move or perhaps see his gray shadow and the VC will lose one man in finding out that the guards here are not fools.

Despite those thoughts, Nuong was afraid and sweating, his skin prickly; he listened. He started staring at something he could barely see—a patch of reeds out past the wall. He could see the tips of them against the dull sky. He reached out for a clacker. Moved the safety bar down. Silently eased onto his stomach and motioned Lemmen to do the same. Closed his eyes, held his breath, squeezed the clacker three times. Even through closed eyelids everything flashed white, and his ears were pierced with pain.

Nuong sprang to his knees and brought up his rifle. He heard a metallic sliding sound and a pop; a small explosion came from Lemmen's lap, a shower of sparks, a whoosh, a wavy trail of white smoke as a flare shot up over the swamp. There it burst into light, crackling like a torch, falling underneath a parachute. It drifted and wavered, lighting up reeds and black water, reeds and black water. Reeds and black water and that was all.

Hoa was doing something dangerous. She knew that as she slipped out the back door and clicked the lock quietly. She picked up her bundle. There was a certain brightness to the night; points of moonlight were reflecting from the waves of the Mekong. Hoa slipped along the dockside, silent, in bare feet, the concrete cold on her soles.

She turned down an alley, walked along a wall, kicked a can in the darkness, which made her cry "Oi!" before she shushed herself, fingers over her mouth. At the end of the alley she stopped to look at the main street. Empty and silent. Merely by stepping out there she would break the curfew law—the QCs would love to arrest her. As they loved to arrest all bar girls. To taunt them about their GI lovers. Sometimes to slap them—some of her friends had been slapped on the street by QCs. And they would want their bribe. As if a military policemen's salary were not enough! As if bar girls were fountains of money.

She slipped out and walked, staying in the moon shadow of the apartment buildings and stores. Everything was still. The perfume of night flowers was mixed with the husky smell of milled rice. She came up to the rice warehouse, spooky in its silence. By day it was trucks and cyclos, huge baskets of rice coming and going; but at night, a silvery-white ghost. Hoa looked behind her. Empty moonlit street, all the way back to the monument and traffic circle.

She hurried past the rice warehouse, past the darkness of the soccer field. In the villages the VC were the danger, but in town her own people—the QCs, the Arvin Rangers —they were the danger. Here, at the edge of town, she felt the hunch coming out of her shoulders. She stuck to the dirt path at the side of the road, where bushes hid her from the moonlight, and she felt the comfort of being almost invisible.

She passed the white ruins of the schoolhouse. Not many years ago it had been the pride of the town, built with money stolen from the Americans, or so the fishwomen had whispered. The province chief had made that an open secret—to impress the townspeople with his resourcefulness. It was money diverted cleverly to a good cause, with some, of course, going into the chief's pocket —he had to survive. But now look. Hardly one brick left on top of another. And why? Because stupid soldiers decided to have a fight over it. Now the children went to school in huts, like primitives. Yes, for everything the Americans had given, they had taken something away.

But she should not say stupid soldiers, because Bill was there. She hadn't met Bill yet; it was years ago and she was the newest bar girl and had been asleep in her room after being handled and teased and breathed on by drunken GIs all night, and she'd barely fallen asleep when booming noises almost knocked her out of bed. It turned out to be GIs, who had found out that rebels were grouping in the schoolhouse at night. Bill was with a whole company of GIs who surprised them in there, shot the schoolhouse to pieces, blew it up with mortars—finally, they won. And ruined the schoolhouse. And killed one rebel, while the others ran away. The dead boy was from two villages down. But the GIs had won. Soldiers called that winning.

She stopped near a grove of banana trees. Not too close, they were full of rats and spiders, those trees. But she used their shadows to stop and listen for traffic. There was so little movement at night, and so much silence, that even in her room Hoa could sometimes hear traffic coming miles away. Now she listened for the distant, whiny pitch of tires—then dashed across the road, the white stripe flying under her feet, bundle bouncing against her leg. She got to the other side, warm Vietnamese dirt under her feet again.

She had grown up on this path. A thousand times she had run to market down this path, with a coin purse jingling and a note from her mother that said, in writing that was almost sculptured, *Give My Daughter One of Your Best Chickens, Not Too Old, And For Not More Than Twelve Piasters.* Twelve piasters! That was a sad joke. A chicken was two hundred fifty piasters, if you could get one. Another thing the GIs had done. They brought money to town but their spending drove up the price of everything. At one time each family raised and ate its own chickens, but then things changed; the villagers started selling their chickens, and buying beef, factory-made blouses, shrimp, and cigarettes. Unlike her uncles and some other villagers, Hoa was not entirely bitter about the changes; after all, people were getting rich, and the coming of the GIs meant the end of her days in the rice paddies.

Here where the path met the main street—the GIs called it Route 4—there was an overgrown ruin. How fast the patches of jungle reclaimed things! Even in the daytime you could hardly see any cinder block. But once it had been a beautiful apartment building, three stories high, fifteen units in all, with balconies open to the night breezes—too open, it turned out.

But once upon a time it was the fanciest apartment building in town, with water pipes, electricity, and TV antennas. Many apartments were occupied by GIs who called themselves MAC-V, although Hoa had never understood, really, what that stood for. Except that those GIs were big spenders in the bars. Also in the apartments were a few American construction workers, the wealthiest men she had ever known. Too wealthy to bother with her; they had the prettiest girls for miles around. On the bottom floor were Vietnamese families who had something to do with MAC-V. She remembered walking past here when she was a teenager and this building was alive with lights and noise. She could tell the apartments where the Americans and their girls lived, because of the loud music and the drunken laughter. She could tell where the Vietnamese families lived too. Because of the arguing, the male voices screaming insults. The sound of something thrown. A slap. A woman crying.

Family life in the village! It was while walking along this road when she was seventeen that she made her plan. She would move to town and become a bar girl. Maybe she would be lucky and find herself a decent GI. If not, she would save to become a fishmonger.

Hoa walked past that ruin toward the darkness of the deeper path. Yes, that apartment building, and something else, was blown to pieces in the Tet fighting of years ago. Until then, most of the townspeople agreed: The GIs can save us; they will hold off the rebels until Saigon and Uncle Ho can agree. After the Tet fighting, even though the government and the GIs had won, the building stayed in ruins, and the fishwomen talked every day of VC's return.

Hoa walked carefully through a tunnel of darkness, trees grown completely over the trail. Beyond the trees on either side were rice paddies and dikes, rice paddies and canals. She was barefoot for silence but also to feel for tripwires. At one time the villagers assumed they were immune to traps laid for the GIs, but they since had learned many hard lessons. The ricelands were filling up with graves. But still the soldiers wouldn't stop. Some crazy boy would get a hand grenade and attach it to a tripwire and not care who came along next. That was the level of things, these days. She felt her way carefully, down her girlhood trail, in bare feet.

In a while she reached her home. It was in a circle of huts in a clearing under the moonlight. None of the homes showed light, except for Mister Ma's home, the nicest in the village, with a tin roof and wood sides. Mister Ma had traveled all the way to France and spoke French and had once been a field supervisor, and was now retired. He had taken a young wife, the old codger, and she had given him a son. Then the wife had run away. Mister Ma and his son were the only ones left in the village now. Five empty huts. Hoa passed Mister Ma's home almost on tiptoes, to avoid any chance of probing and needling. Where has your mother gone, Miss Muon? I'm surprised she left after being appointed a Patriot Mother. She was the last one I would have thought would desert us for Saigon.

There was no door, never had been. The home was built of poles, with walls of bamboo weave, and straw on the roof. Outside were two big jars to collect rainwater, and Hoa dipped her hand in, cupped it, brought it to her lips. Sweet and cool.

She entered the house thinking: Hello, Mother. It would seem somehow that her mother would always be here. But moonlight coming in the window showed her an empty home, except for one trunk. She put her bundle on it. Unrolled it quietly.

Just one big room, that was all they'd ever had, and they grew up sleeping, the four of them, on their dining table, on bedrolls. Her father long dead of a stomach disease. Her little brother now a hard-faced QC in Can Tho. Who had not spoken to her since she became a bar girl. But what was she to do? There were no Vietnamese men left, even if she'd wanted one. All the meanness she had endured for daring to move to town!

But the dining-sleeping table was gone now. She

smoothed her bedroll out on the dirt floor. It was a bit frightening because of snakes, on a cool night they searched out the warmth of a sleeping body. So she did not undress. Made herself lie down, and tried not to think of things. She listened in the dark. Footsteps? No, it must be her heartbeat. She closed her eyes and breathed in slowly. From somewhere came the drawn-out chirp of a house lizard. Which put Hoa at peace. It would not be a night at home without that birdlike chirp. They were cute, for lizards, and kept a home bug-free and children made a game of capturing them. If you grabbed their tails they would detach them, escape, and grow new ones. Hoa always liked that idea.

There was a shushing sound; someone had struck a match but before Hoa opened her eyes she heard someone say: Who is in this home?

I am, Mister Ma, Hoa Muon. She sat up.

You, said Mister Ma. His face and white chin beard were illuminated by the flame. It went out and he struck another match, held it out.

It is you. I heard someone come by. What do you hear from your mother, miss?

She is safely in Saigon, Hoa said. I have a letter. She felt around among her things. Mister Ma lit a tiny candle. Squatted and set it between them.

She found the envelope—the right envelope—and held it up for Mister Ma to see. He took it. He was the village elder and had every right to read it.

Why have you come back here? Mister Ma said. It is dangerous for a girl to travel at night.

You will understand when you read the letter, Hoa said.

Mister Ma grunted. He read. He was wearing a striped nightgown that was like silk and had been bought in Paris, or so he told everyone. The slippers on his old spotted feet weren't a peasant's rubber thongs but soft brown leather.

I see your mother has come to her senses where you are concerned, Mister Ma said. He handed the letter back to

Hoa. This she should have done years ago. And she is right! When those northerners get their hands on people like you with your English and me with my French, we'd better pretend we know nothing. I agree with your mother's orders for you. You must especially stay away from that bar. Distance yourself from it. Quit your job at the base. Become a peasant girl! Peasants are neutral, everyone knows that. And for God's sake why did you come at night?

So no one would see me, Hoa said.

Unmarried girls, Mister Ma said, there's no sense in them. He looked at her. His voice became softer. And you, sleeping in your clothes, are you?

Hoa drew back and shifted on her bedroll. Crossed her arms in front of her stomach. I was very tired, she said. I have worked all day.

If you call that work, Mister Ma said.

Hoa took the insult and said nothing.

Maybe you ought to come sleep in my house, Mister Ma said.

Hoa shook her head. My mother wants me to stay here, she said, until my brother comes for me.

Since when are you obedient? Mister Ma said. He stood up. Smoothed his pajamas. Blew out his candle. You are very headstrong, miss, he said. Give my regards to your mother when you go up there. Tell her old Mister Ma, at least, is standing his ground.

I will, said Hoa. So he would go away. When he shuffled off, she lifted her rear off the bedroll and yes, she had managed to sit on it, and hide it from Mister Ma. Another envelope, but this one with no stamp. She put it inside her blouse and lay down to a restless sleep.

Pots and Pans

Lemmen woke up with a hangover, reached for his canteen, gulped warm water. Already it was bright and steamy in the tent, and Lemmen, who had slept fully dressed against the mosquitoes, was sweating out the bourbon of last night's guard duty.

He grabbed his carbine and crawled to daylight. Saw Nuong sleeping on a poncho in the shade of the ammo crates. The camp people were gathered around a smoky fire; the air smelled of barbecued meat. There were more wives and kids than soldiers, and Lemmen remembered why: During his last hour of guard, they had sent out a dawn patrol. A noisy dawn patrol, the soldiers carrying pots and pans tied to their waists. Lemmen wondered about that, gave it up. Then he thought about trying to find Van, and getting his radio back. But something more urgent took him to the mud wall at the edge of the compound. Where he let out last night's bourbon and water into the swamp.

He had finished, buttoned up, and lit a Lucky when he saw Van in the swamp, standing on a spit of mud, sur-

rounded by black water. Lemmen slung his carbine, strad-
dled the wall, and went over it. Walked squishy-foot
through mud, water, and grass.

The boy saw him coming, grinned, and gave a big wave
of one hand. He wore the same white shirt, same raggy
pants. When Lemmen got close, he noticed, at the kid's
bare feet, a beat-up galvanized tin bucket with a woven
bamboo cover.

"You!" Van shouted to Lemmen.

"*Chao,*" Lemmen said. "Radio. Mine. Me."

Van shrugged, showed his empty hands and grinned.

"Look, I'll give it to you when I leave," Lemmen said,
and then realized Van couldn't understand. "Tomorrow,"
he said. "Today, radio me. Tomorrow, radio you. You *bic*?"

The boy shook his head.

Lemmen put a purposeful scowl on his face, leaned in
toward the boy, raised his voice. "Radio. Me. Now!"

Van backed off, but only a half step. He hadn't stopped
grinning. He bent to his bucket, lifted the cover, and
looked in, a real alertness in his eyes. His hand made a
quick move into the bucket, pulled right back. He waited
and watched. Made another grab and came up with a
snake. A skinny snake three feet long, red with black
rings. He held it behind the head. It did not squirm.

"You like?" Van asked.

"Nice," said Lemmen.

"Number one. You like?" he said, and held the snake
toward Lemmen.

"No, no," Lemmen said, and stepped back.

"Radio me," Van said, and held out the snake.

Then Lemmen got it: the offer of a trade; one radio for
one snake. That was fair—well, not quite. "I don't need a
pet right now," he said, and looked in the bucket. It was
full of writhing snakes. He suddenly made a connection:
the smoky fire, the barbecue smell, the snakes in the
bucket; Van was offering him breakfast.

"No like," Lemmen said.

Van shrugged. He wrapped the snake around his neck.

"Hey!" Lemmen said. "Cut that out. Put it back in the bucket." Van grinned, took the snake from around his neck, and held it at arm's length toward Lemmen. It started to writhe.

"No!" Lemmen said.

"Okay," Van said. He lifted the bamboo cover and spiraled the snake in as if it were a rope. None of the snakes tried to escape. All were tangled in a giant knot. Van dropped the cover back in place.

"This is the same kid who won't eat C rations," Lemmen said—a joke to himself. Then he had a somber thought: These people have to catch snakes if they want to eat; they are really abandoned. They don't even get rations from Saigon—maybe a few sacks of rice. He found himself staring at Van's feet. He walks barefoot in this water? Lemmen asked himself. Knowing how many snakes are in there? He told himself that Van was the kind of kid who grew up to be VC. A kid who would walk barefoot through smelly, leech-ridden, snake-infested water, grab a snake, throw it in a bucket, eat it for breakfast. Whatever gave Americans the idea they could defeat such people?

Van bent over and pulled on a thin rope, and a bamboo cage rose out of black water. He fixed bait—some kind of chopped fish—into a split piece of bamboo inside the cage. Then threw the cage back and watched it sink. Bubbles burst on the slimy surface, releasing foul air. Lemmen had done some crabbing as a kid, when he'd lived for one humid summer in South Carolina, but he could not figure out how the cage trapped snakes. He wished he had learned to speak something more than whorehouse Vietnamese.

Van, done with his baiting, came up and shook Lemmen's hand, kept it up, as if he would never stop. He said, "Okay," once for each shake.

"You're okay, too, Van," Lemmen said. The boy's hand was slimy. Lemmen tried to keep any reaction off his face.

Van kept shaking his hand. "You number one, you," he said.

"You too, Van," Lemmen said.

"You say lem me," Van said.

"No get Salems," Lemmen said. Finally, Van was through shaking his hand. Lemmen resisted the urge to wipe the slime off on his trousers. *"Xin loi,"* he said. "Salem. No get. You . . ." He pointed at Van. "Radio me."

"No get," Van said. He picked up his bucket and started to walk away. Every few steps he turned around to shout, "Okay," at Lemmen and make a circle out of his thumb and forefinger. Lemmen watched him go. Van climbed over the mud wall, disappeared with his bucket of snakes.

Lemmen lit another Lucky and, his mouth sour already, promised himself that someday soon he would quit smoking. Maybe after this mission. Suddenly he saw something big moving out in the reeds. He whipped his rifle off his shoulder, went into a crouch, flicked the safety off, touched the trigger. Out of the reeds came the Arvin patrol, wading down a stream.

They were carrying something, it looked like a pig on a spit. But Lemmen couldn't recall hearing any shooting. Maybe he'd been asleep.

The soldiers climbed a flimsy bridge made of sticks, crossed a river of deep black water, and went toward the wall. Lemmen realized they were not carrying a pig. They were talking among themselves, high and fast.

Now he was sure of what he saw: a body tied to a bamboo pole. The Arvins moved up to the wall with it. The body, dressed only in shorts, was tied by its ankles and wrists, the head dropped way back. The soldiers climbed the wall, there was a lot of shouting and direction giving. When they lifted the body over, the pots and pans hanging from their belts clanked. Across the compound, the women and children waited as if behind some boundary; the Dai-ui came hard strides for the wall.

Lemmen was drawn toward this thing. He followed the

Arvin stragglers and watched as the Dai-ui shouted a halt to the patrol and the soldiers dropped the body—it flopped in the mud.

The Dai-ui nudged the body with his foot. He said something angry to the soldiers that made them all look at each other and shuffle. The women and children edged closer. The Dai-ui shouted something at a sergeant, then raised his command stick and pointed out at the swamp.

Already flies buzzed the body. Which was bloated; it had been in the water a few hours. A shiver went through Lemmen and he felt very small. As he stared at the body he realized it had a black stain for a face.

Then he noticed Van coming through the crowd. Van wriggled past the Dai-ui's legs, stopped inches short of the body. He looked across at Lemmen, pointed at the body and shouted, "VC." Then he brought his leg back and kicked the body. The Dai-ui snapped out a curse, and Van gave him a sideways look. The Dai-ui slapped his stick at the boy, who twisted away and scrambled over to Lemmen. "VC," he said. "You crackadau VC." He put out his hand for Lemmen to shake.

Lemmen put one hand in his hip pocket and with the other, took off his boonie hat, fanned the sweat off his face. He looked out at the swamp; it steamed like a giant flat kettle of soup. He let his mind wander north, imagined himself tomorrow night in a bar on Tu Do Street, drinking a cold Monkey, two young ladies in the booth with him. He could see the red Naugahyde of the booth, he could hear "Hey, Good Lookin' " on the jukebox, he could taste the yeasty unsterilized beer. The young ladies would speak fractured English, ask for Saigon Teas, their long fingernails moving cleverly on his thigh. They would be over-made-up, spoiled city girls, with the hardest hearts— not like Hoa at all. But then, they didn't ask you to marry them, they were happy with five hundred piasters and a few Saigon Teas.

Lemmen leaned on ammo crates; in front of him the mortar tube gleamed, silver in the sun. He'd met his goal for the morning. He'd opened the top layer of ammo crates, slipped the rounds out, pulled safety pins, ripped off charge bags. He was still sweating hard—but soon,

when Command landed with a chopper full of VIPs, he
would be nothing less than full strack cavalry. Had to be,
if he wanted his chance to stay in-country.

He picked up a round, ripped off two charge bags. The
mud at his feet was littered with the yellow bags, filled
with gunpowder. He looked over at the next mortar,
where Nuong was giving a talk to a group of Arvins. He
tried to think how he would explain charge bags. He tried
the simple: The more charge bags on a round, the farther
it will go. But, hell, most of them would already know
that. He needed a formula. Something snappy they'd remember in the panic of firing. He stripped charge bags
and thought it over.

He wiped sweat from his face again. These were the
worst kinds of days; by midmorning you could barely
breathe. He took his canteen from a shady spot at the base
of ammo crates. Sipped hot water. What he wouldn't pay
for a cold Elephant. At this point, even a Budweiser. He
looked around at the work he had done. Crates stacked
chest-high, a perfect horseshoe around the mortar. The
long-distance rounds, with all charge bags intact, were at
the left part of the horseshoe. The short rounds, a few
charge bags pulled from each, were on the right. Illumes
in the middle. They were ready for anything, Lemmen
felt. Could pin down a whole battalion. Especially in a
swamp—no place to dig in.

He fanned himself with his hat. Which must have
weighed a pound. The big thing on Lemmen's hat, on top,
was a 9th Cavalry unit patch, depicting a flying black eagle
with a sword in its talons. Pinned just below that, a P-38
can opener. Here and there, black safety pins, the kind
that came with ammo bandoliers. Stuck in the headband
was a tiny white Buddha carved out of a tiger's tooth, a
dozen rusting grenade rings, a pack of Luckies, the Zippo,
a plastic capsule of mortarman's earplugs he never used, a
tiny American-flag lapel pin, a miniature compass, and his
rank, a three-striped chevron. Lemmen put the hat down,

took a cigarette out of the pack. The air was so damp that the cigarette was limp, the white paper speckled with wet tobacco stains.

He lit the cigarette, then stopped to listen. Did he hear something in the sky? Strange how you could hear helicopters so far away. Not hear them, actually. It was something at the edge of hearing and intuition. He scanned the sky. Nothing but haze. Looked at his Lucky and it had gone out. He flipped up the cover of the Zippo for a relight when he definitely heard something: a crackle on the radio, his call sign, one-niner. Before he could turn for the radio, he heard, faint but unmistakable, the pop-pop-pop of rotor blades.

He shouted Nuong's name and waved for him to come over. Then crouched in the drying mud in front of the radio, picked up the mike, and said, "This is one-niner," and waited for an answer. He looked up and the helicopter appeared; it was high, coming out of the sun. Around the mortar, Nuong gathered a scraggly cluster of Arvin soldiers.

Lemmen repeated his call, the helicopter dropping in on them fast, and Command's voice said on the radio: "We're bringing in our Victor Inca Papas. What stage of the lesson are you in at this time? Over."

Lemmen pushed the talk button. "Almost ready to fire the first round, sir," he said. Couldn't quite catch himself. Not supposed to mention rank on the radio.

"Hold your fire until we're on the ground."

"Roger," Lemmen said, and came out of his crouch. He stood next to Nuong, who, like a human blackboard, held up the big plastic plotting wheel. Where with dots and arcs drawn in melting crayon, Lemmen, in slow English, started to explain the geometry of mortar fire. Pausing every sentence so Nuong could translate. The Dai-ui had come up to stand behind his soldiers, his command stick tapping his boot. He whipped one soldier across the back of the calves for laughing.

The chopper started a circling descent, and to compete with the noise, Lemmen raised his voice. "So as I was saying, by using this wheel you will quickly calculate the deflection in mils." He stopped and listened to Nuong's translation. Of which he understood maybe two words.

"The mils are always read off in four digits," Lemmen said. "The whole point is," he said, in an even louder voice, "that you've already set up the mortar for a known direction . . ." He paused, walked out toward the first aiming stake. He consulted his compass, fingered the binoculars hanging from his neck. Had he lost his students already? Nuong's translation went out to Arvins; most of them stared at the ground. "Since you know that one direction," Lemmen said, "the plotting wheel will tell you how much to move the mortar to hit any target. That's called the deflection." During the translation he walked back to the mortar tube. "You set the deflection in mils here on the mortar sight, move the gun until the aiming stakes are in the cross hairs of your sight . . ." He wondered about the concept of deflection. Was he getting it across? He bent to look through the sight; the aiming posts were almost exactly in the cross hairs. "Just requires a little adjustment," Lemmen said, and shoved the gun almost imperceptibly. "I've drawn a picture of the aiming process, and Sergeant Nuong will pass that around later." For some infraction that Lemmen missed, a soldier got tapped on the shoulder by the Dai-ui's stick.

"Now . . ." Lemmen said. He'd raised his voice to shouting; the helicopter had dropped to a hundred feet, circling. He paused for a moment, overcome by the paranoid idea that Nuong was translating something else entirely, making fun of him. He tried to make eye contact with the Arvins, no success. In the back rank somewhere an Arvin giggled.

"You must now call the deflection, range, and elevation to the gunner," Lemmen shouted, and turned his back on the soldiers, called numbers to Nuong, who put down the plotting board, came over and cranked the handle, raising the angle of the gun. "And now we are ready to fire," Lemmen said. He looked out toward the clump of trees where yesterday they had sent their first practice round. Had that round, by blind fate, killed the VC scout whose body was now covered with field jackets at the edge of the compound? Or had Nuong gotten him last night with the claymore? Forward, Lemmen told himself. Cavalry. Either way, it was murder, a voice inside him said. Cavalry! He told himself. Forward! It was him or us!

The helicopter feathered into a hover over the middle of the camp; it made a hot wind that stank of jet fuel. No one could speak or be heard over the ferocious chop of the rotor. The helicopter bounced once on its skids and set down. The whine of the engine faded and the blades slowed, then stopped with a final tweet. The chopper's flashing red light turned; everything else stayed still.

What a chopper it was! All shiny with Turtle Wax. The Plexiglas windows clear and uncracked. The body without a single bullet hole, scrape, or missing rivet. Painted on the fuselage was a 9th Cavalry eagle, five feet high, a gleam in the bird's eye. Lemmen wondered where Command had found such a chopper; there sure weren't any like it at Delta Town.

The doorgunners unfixed M-60s and stepped out holding them, linked to the helicopter by the chain of brassy ammo; the gunners wore helmets, with the green sun visors down—they looked like invaders from another planet. Lemmen waited for Command or maybe the VIPs to climb out. Nobody moved but the gunners.

Lemmen stared into the cabin of the chopper but could not see Command. In one canvas seat sat an old man in striped pants and a safari shirt; a thin, half-bald man with white hair, his arms resting on the sides of his seat. Beside him, crouching, talking straight into his ear, and holding a clipboard, was a tall, slender, gray-haired woman in starched combat fatigues. Lemmen finally saw Command in the copilot's seat.

Nobody moved. The gunners stood at something like attention, their guns pointed at the swamp. The old man and the woman stayed in the cabin, the woman still talking into the old man's ear. It was very quiet. The red light kept flashing. The Arvins stared at the chopper.

It was hypnosis, broken by the crack of an opening door, and Command stepping out. He crossed the mud toward them, his hand out. He went first to the Dai-ui, saluted, and then shook his hand. "Congratulations," he said to the Dai-ui, and then came to Lemmen and shook his hand, nodding to Nuong. "You're doing a fine job here, Sergeants," he said. He lowered his voice and said to Lemmen: "Come on up for a ride."

The introductions were made and Lemmen pretended he
could hear them; as if you could hear anything inside a
slick while it was taking off. The congressman, whoever
he was, pretended too—he smiled nicely, offered his hand,
then drew his head back. Which made Lemmen realize
how bad he must smell. The woman put on a flight helmet
and gave him a limp hand and a smile that didn't show
much tooth. They were up a thousand feet before Lemmen, finished with the amenities, strapped himself into
the canvas jump seat.

The crew chief gave Lemmen his helmet; the chief's
face was hard, his hair shaved to a nubby crewcut. He
could have been twenty-five, he could have been forty. A
half-moon scar ran the length of his lower lip, and when
he tried to smile at Lemmen it came out a scowl. Lemmen
put the helmet on; for a moment he was an insider, hearing the cross talk between the pilot and Command. The
chopper reached altitude and turned, hovered, giving
Lemmen a view of the swampy serpentine trail that led to
Cambodia.

Command's staticky voice came into the helmet. "Ma'am, Sergeant, you with me?" Lemmen said, "Yes, sir," into the tiny microphone at his lips; the woman's reply, if any, was lost.

"Now look straight out there," Command said, "and you'll see what I'm talking about. What looks like a stream —that thing leads right over the border. Charley's got a name for that stream: Victory Highway, he calls it. Well, we'll just see about that."

The helicopter bounced and dipped and shook, struggling to hold still. It was so much cooler up there, such a relief; the air felt like it does at a mountain retreat.

"Now, at high tide that's a stream," Command said, "but at low tide it becomes a path, and you can move an army down it. It's the only way through the swamp—'less, of course, you want to lose half your men to drowning. When Charley comes at us, it's going to be at low tide, down that path. If he wants to go to Saigon, he's going to have to take the left fork, and fight the Arvins every mile."

The woman was nodding; she had her visor up and was listening intently, as far as Lemmen could tell. "We're going to fight Charley until he decides to take that right fork, going toward the Mekong. Once he gets to the river, there's a village, and of course he'll steal fishing boats— there'll be lots of fishing boats—and he'll cross the river. Then he'll be ours. We're going to deflect them down that right fork, on purpose, ma'am, and that's why our sergeant here is going to lead a little ambush on that trail tonight."

Lemmen looked across into the woman's eyes; they were as gray as her hair. He couldn't get a read on her. Did she think he was a patriot, a hero, a fool?

The chopper rose and started to circle. "Sergeant Lemmen, would you be kind enough to pass your helmet over to the honorable congressman at this time?"

Lemmen took it off. Unstrapped himself, grabbed a pole, leaned over the shifting metal floor, put the helmet in the old man's lap. It took the old man maybe three seconds to realize it was there and grab it. Lemmen wasn't sure, but he thought the congressman could have been napping. He sat down and strapped himself in again.

Whatever the conversation, he was out of it now, and all he could do was look. As the chopper climbed higher he could see the round hazy purple lumps of the Seven Sisters—which got him thinking about what led him to Vinh Long in the first place, and then to disaster at the foot of those mountains.

It began in Little America. Lemmen had only been in-country four days when he met First Sergeant Worthington—big, flabby, the palest kind of white man, bald except for fringes of flame-red hair, fifty years old, a guy who could have easily retired, but for some reason wouldn't. Even back then, in 1969, Worthington was on his third tour of the Republic. He liked his vodka plenty and undiluted, and, if you believed the nastiest rumors—Lemmen didn't—spent his off-duty time on Tu Do Street in the company of effeminate Vietnamese boys.

They met on adjacent barstools at the NCO club. Neither of them was close to sober. Worthington, no doubt noticing the deep newbie-green of Lemmen's uniform, started giving advice: New in-country, I take it? Never been here before? Listen, don't be scared of this place. This isn't a war anymore, it's a damn game. Army itself can't even understand that. But Sergeant, the army's no smarter than its dumbest noncom—and that's pretty dumb. Listen up! I'll tell you what you got to watch out for . . .

A half hour later, Worthington had stopped talking to search his wallet for more MPC, and Lemmen got in a few complaints about Fort Carson, his last duty station. Worthington, not really listening, looked him over as if he'd just then seen him; he said he had a slot for an E-6, needed a big guy with a booming bass voice. And then, after just a few questions, offered Lemmen a job reading the newbie manifests.

For the next week, Lemmen was dazzled by his own luck. He would be in a war zone, where a soldier belonged, but he would never have to hump the boonies—he could sleep every night in the luxury of Little America. In a real bunk. And all around him, movie theaters, hamburger stands, swimming pools, massage parlors, and that magnificent NCO club—and just outside the gate was the war.

They issued him an M-16 to keep in his locker and he knew what that meant—he had arrived. No more mickey mouse! His assignment was to sit in an air-conditioned tower, overlooking an asphalt square the size of a basketball court. All he had to do was read the names of newbies, followed by their unit assignments, from sheafs of computer paper. The newbies stood below, in their dark green uniforms, waiting to hear their in-country fates. Day after day Lemmen's voice boomed out of a bank of speakers. Seven to nine in the morning, three to five in the afternoon. Easiest duty of Lemmen's career. Seven days a week, that was the only drawback.

It didn't seem like much of a drawback until maybe the second month. By then Lemmen was bored with Little America, and craving Vietnam. Little America, he felt, could have been a crude shopping mall in, say, Georgia. Except for the night sirens—usually false alarms—and the occasional far-off Cobra firefight, it seemed they were nowhere near a war. Lemmen started hitchhiking down to Tu Do Street in between shifts—to get a taste of the real thing.

For the first few days he just roamed the alleys, which were jammed with peddlers selling orange soda, Seiko watches, prerolled marijuana cigarettes, jade jewelry, military medals and patches, ice-cream bars, cameras, carved walking sticks, bags of noodles, tubular pillows, sausages-on-sticks, loafers and sneakers, rice cakes, chess sets, bronze statuary, photo scrapbooks, ivory statuary, black-light posters, peace symbols, blue jeans, cassette tapes.

The city was hot and exotic, dirty and crowded, beautiful and dangerous; it looked like a tropical Paris. On the boulevards, the windows of every hotel, bank, and restaurant were covered by grenade screens; sandbags and steel gates were everywhere. QCs and MPs prowled in jeeps, M-16s ready. In the alleys, lepers and amputees begged for coins. Whores beckoned from every bar; from doorways, opium peddlers advertised by forming their fingers into O's; teenage boys shouted "short-time" from windows, pimping their younger sisters; Saigon cowboys raced by on cyclos, ripping watches off arms, cameras off necks.

Back at Little America, the newbies' names and assignments all sounded the same. The movies changed only once a month, the swimming pool smelled like pure chlorine, the club served nothing but Budweiser, the hamburgers were always burnt to a tasteless lump. The closest thing to sex was a five-dollar hand job at the massage parlor, and the brass wanted to stop even that.

Sometime in there Lemmen became a patron of the Butterfly Bar. It was at the mouth of one the dirtier alleys, and was red inside: red Naugahyde, red wallpaper, red carpet—the light bulbs were orange. When Lemmen lit a Lucky in there, the glowing tip of it was nearly invisible.

First he met Sharon and then he met Sue. Or was it the other way around? Sharon had bad teeth; Sue had a diagonal scar across her neck. Neither of them spoke good English. His second Saturday night in there, Lemmen decided he could afford both of them; who knew, he told himself, when he'd ever be in a place like this again, wide open, where an ordinary guy could afford the best bottle of whiskey, a nice hotel room, and two young ladies willing to do anything.

On Sunday he woke up alone, dry and in pain—it was afternoon, the desk clerk rapping on the door, shouting for another day's rent. Lemmen paid it, and later in Little

America paid the ninety-dollar fine for being AWOL, and swore to himself and to Worthington that he had seen the last of the Butterfly Bar.

But on Wednesday he found himself back there for a lunchtime quickie with Sharon and on Thursday for lunch he had three bourbons and Sue and on Friday night he started a two-day bender; when he reported to Worthington on Monday, he got another ninety-dollar fine, and a lecture from Worthington. Who said: I know it's fun downtown, Sergeant, I'd stay there myself three hundred sixty-five days a year—if I could. But I can't, and neither can you. Unless, of course, you have some kind of abnormal desire to hump the boonies.

The threat kept Lemmen on base for two weeks. For which he rewarded himself by going back down to Tu Do Street, for one Saturday night drink and a couple of feels —it ended up in a five-day drunk, sometimes with Sharon, sometimes with Sue, sometimes wandering strange alleys alone. He only sobered up when he lost his wallet and went back to Little America—this time it was out of Worthington's hands; Lemmen pleaded guilty at a summary court-martial that lasted less than five minutes.

He got busted to E-4, lost his job, and Worthington, furious at having to do the court-martial paperwork, transferred him to the Delta; You're lucky I'm not sending you to the DMZ, Worthington said.

Before he went down to the Delta, he had to do thirty days KP at the Little America jail. He had plenty of time to think while scrubbing pots and pans. The pots were big enough to cook a hog in. Lemmen, with soap, a brush, and a hose, outdoors at the back of a stinking kitchen, scrubbed and scoured pot after pan, twelve hours a day, until his hands bled. His boots were constantly soaked, everything smelled of cold grease. Tu Do Street, he'd since found out, translated to Liberty Street, maybe too much liberty. A soldier was born for hardship and discipline, he told himself. Without the discipline of the army, a soldier was a drunken, dangerous, sorry whorechaser. Without the hardship of war, a soldier was a pathetic boot-polishing paper-pusher. Life was sorrow—KP made him realize that. Dishwater and filthy pots—this was real. Bourbon and Sharon and Sue—they were lies. Often, with his elbows sunk in suds, or with a pot and a brush in his hands, Lemmen found himself remembering, without bitterness, all the failings of his father.

He had four hours between the end of his KP tour and the flight to the Delta, and he used it to look up Worthington, and apologize. Worthington said he understood about this country, how it had things that could lead a man astray. He said he liked Lemmen and hoped he would get straight. Then they walked to the NCO club, where Lemmen had his first drink in five weeks.

The bartender was a girl of maybe seventeen, and after a few drinks Lemmen was getting horny for her. She had a slit skirt and her name was Marilyn and he could have fallen in love with her right there, but he had his new resolve; besides, he was going down to the Delta, to be in a grunt squad and hopefully win his sergeant's stripes back; he told Worthington he was looking forward to that, but he could barely keep his eyes off Marilyn and then he looked at his watch and had to run woozy for his flight.

That was how the crooked trail of his career led him to Delta Town, and the Seven Sisters, and when he looked out the helicopter's door to catch another glimpse of those sorry purple hills, he found himself thinking about Buck Shannon and Worthington and Earl Holloway and Jimmy Carney and his old man—all the ghosts of his life.

The Dai-ui stood beside the body, which was covered by three muddy field jackets; hundreds of flies buzzed it in the midday heat. The Dai-ui pointed at the body, pointed at where the helicopter had disappeared into the sky. Where have they gone? the Dai-ui demanded. What are they doing up there? When are they going to take away this thing? He kicked at the body. The flies rose in a cloud, settled back down.

They are showing some officials around, Nuong said.

When they come back, will they take this rebel off my hands? the Dai-ui asked.

I don't think so, Nuong said.

Lovely, the Dai-ui said. Suppose his comrades decide to liberate the body! These Americans fly off like tourists and leave us stuck. When are they going back to Saigon? I myself would like to go to Saigon. I would like to check on my mother. I would like to see how my brothers are doing —one of them's with the tax office now, you know. He might have the ear of someone important. He might be able to get me reassigned to Saigon. Away from this mud-hole. I am no swamp rat, Sergeant, I have family all over the capital. The least Major Hopkins could have done was take me up with him. Then perhaps I could have persuaded him to take me to Saigon. Only for a few days—on military business.

I don't believe they're going to Saigon, Nuong said. I believe they are going to the Cambodian border.

Let them! I have enough troubles here in this cesspool. Cambodia. It's bad enough we're this close. Who would want to get any closer? Why, if I had command of a helicopter, I would fly it right up to the capital. Never mind this swamp. Why are they going to Cambodia?

I have no idea, Nuong said.

Wouldn't you rather go to Saigon?

Yes. I, too, have my family in that area, Nuong said.

Oh? the Dai-ui said. What district?

Well, not in the capital exactly—Bien Hoa.

Oh, up there, the Dai-ui said. Well, I suppose it is nice in a smaller place. Of course, it is no small place anymore, with all those planes and helicopters. I wonder how the people sleep! But, Nuong, really, I must talk seriously with Major Hopkins when that helicopter comes back—if it comes back. That's what I don't understand about these people, Nuong, they're always rushing into dangerous places. Cambodia! It sends shivers up my spine. Another thing I'd really like, Nuong, is if Major Hopkins would use his helicopter to take this specimen back to the morgue.

I don't think so, Captain, Nuong said. You see, they have big officials from the United States on board. But I will ask if you want me to. Perhaps Sergeant Lemmen could help our case.

That one! the Dai-ui said, and spit off to the side. His idea of strategy is to fire flares on a night when—when there are five thousand NVA looking on. Why didn't he light up the camp and send our coordinates to them?

He is an American, Nuong said, and that is the way they do things.

Apparently. They are such baboons, the Dai-ui said. Don't you agree, Nuong?

Nuong disagreed with the Dai-ui by not answering and looking away. He pretended to scan the swamp as if he were expecting to see something. Really, he had come to know the Big People, and they had a certain nature. They did not reflect, they were not careful to seek all opinions, they just ran off and did things. Nuong had no hope or even desire to change them. But it was useless to try to explain to the Dai-ui what it had taken years of living in America to learn.

Nuong often had the feeling that he no longer belonged anywhere; no matter how good his English or how much time he spent with GIs, he would never be American, and in a camp like this he knew he was considered something of a traitor—as if living in America had ruined him as a loyal Vietnamese. He felt like the monkey in the middle, a game he had seen children play in the United States. One child was the monkey and ran back and forth wearing himself out foolishly while the other two players held a ball until the monkey had it almost in his grasp, then flicked it away.

The Dai-ui took a step and stood face-to-face with him again. When Major Hopkins returns, the Dai-ui said, let's see if we can persuade him to at least take away his "advisor." We don't need any advice! We don't need to go on any ambush. It's dangerous enough staying in camp. Do these Americans think we're going to win the war by ourselves?

He looked in Nuong's eyes, then looked toward the swamp. Maybe if we're lucky and stay quiet, he said, the whole thing will pass us by. Don't you think there's a chance of that, Nuong? Let's not give the rebels any reason to hit us. Imagine if they overran us, Nuong. I have women and children here.

The Dai-ui put a cigarette in his lips. Nuong looked him over: a round man with fat cheeks, wearing a ridiculous black cavalry hat; he was too fat to be an infantryman. He was bad-tempered enough to be an officer, all right, and was good with a swagger stick—but not mean enough for combat. The Dai-ui's hands trembled so badly trying to light his cigarette that the match went out, and Nuong thought: He is no fool, at least. The Dai-ui lit a second match and steadied the tremor, both hands holding it up to the Salem. Nuong, out of courtesy, looked away, but not before he noticed the pinky of this Captain Loan's right hand, with its inch-long tapered fingernail. So, Nuong thought, he is fallen middle class.

I must offer you a Salem, the Dai-ui said.

I have a few cigarettes of my own, thank you.

Are they Salems? the Dai-ui said.

No, Nuong admitted. Even Americans cannot get them now. The PX has been closed for months.

Go ahead, take one of mine, my pleasure, the Dai-ui said.

Nuong accepted; the Dai-ui's pack was nearly empty, the cigarette bent and crumpled. Nuong lit up and inhaled. No other cigarette tasted so good—like candy. He savored that first puff.

Have you ever thought of this, Nuong? the Dai-ui said. Those officials who are riding with Major Hopkins, they are certain to be going to Saigon sometime. Isn't that right? Perhaps I should go along—offer some insights on the way, as to the conduct of the war. I have two excellent lieutenants who could handle anything here. Besides, if anything were to happen, I'm sure Major Hopkins would call in the Cobras. Now—do you think you could talk to your American friend over there . . . What is his name again?

Lemmen, Nuong said.

Yes, the Dai-ui said. He is a very big one, isn't he? If he were in our army, he'd be a two-star general; he would have kicked everybody's ass. But in their army, they don't work by kicking ass, do they?

No, by kissing ass, Nuong said.

Oh, yes, the Dai-ui said, that is a good one, Nuong. The Dai-ui grinned, two big gold teeth. So that's how they work it. Can you persuade that oversize sergeant to talk to Major Hopkins and get me aboard?

Nuong tried to puff on his Salem, but it had gone out. I could try, he said.

Yes, well, the Dai-ui said, the sooner the better. He looked into the sky, but there was no helicopter within sight or sound. I will be in my tent, the Dai-ui said. He looked down at the body. We'll have to get rid of that fellow somehow, Nuong. We can't bury him.

He went off with a salute and Nuong watched him go, then walked toward the middle of the camp. It was hot, the heat was like pressure, the mists had burnt off, the mud had dried to cracked earth. Nuong kept his head down, boots kicking up dust. He thought about the Dai-ui's gold teeth—they marked him for torture if the NVA should ever capture him.

He thought about the Arvin and what bad shape it was in, to need officers like Captain Loan. But what else could be expected, when it was all family and religion and politics—becoming an Arvin officer was no different from getting any other job. Connections were the important thing. In that way, the American army was superior. But they, too, lacked something—why had they failed to beat down the rebels? Why didn't they fly a hundred magnificent Cobras to Cambodia and cut the NVA to pieces? It would take perhaps a day. But no, the Big People wanted the Arvin soldiers to prove themselves. What sense did that make? If the Arvin were any good, they wouldn't need a foreign army to help them. Didn't the Big People understand that?

Nuong held his bent cigarette up for inspection. It had a

break in the paper; no use relighting it. He looked over his shoulder and, sure that the Dai-ui could not see him, dropped the cigarette into the dust and ground it with his boot.

It was dark, and Sergeant Nuong stood with his M-16 strapped over his shoulder and an ammo bandolier tied tight at his waist. Heat lightning flashed over Cambodia somewhere, and the swamp, briefly brilliant, flashed back to shadowy moonlight.

He and Lemmen were waiting for the Dai-ui, who was still rounding up his men. Nuong could hear, from the middle of the compound, bursts of argument, whips of the Dai-ui's command stick. The Dai-ui was supposed to have met Nuong and Lemmen at the stick bridge just after sunset, bringing at least thirty soldiers—none of whom, Nuong was sure, wanted to go. Well, they would be forced to go, because this was an ambush ordered by Major Hopkins and Colonel Tho together, and unless the Dai-ui wanted to personally search for land mines on the DMZ, he would assemble those men.

But he would be in the foulest mood. Because this afternoon Major Hopkins had crushed his hopes for escaping to Saigon: when the helicopter had returned, it hovered just low enough for Sergeant Lemmen to jump out, then took off. The Dai-ui had gone into a cursing fit that lasted fifteen minutes, had stomped through the compound slashing at everything with his stick, and the soldiers, women, and children had scattered to hide in their tents.

The heat lightning flashed, far off, and Nuong heard Lemmen say: "Coming yet?"

"I don't think so," Nuong said. He could see only the shadow of Lemmen, putting one foot on the mud wall, tying his bootlaces. It was perhaps the fourth or fifth time he had done this in the last few minutes. He bloused one trouser leg, tied it tight enough to make him grunt, then did the same to the other leg. "We ought to get out there way before low tide," Lemmen said.

"The Dai-ui knows this," Nuong said.

Which brought from Lemmen only silence. In the faintest lightning flicker, Nuong saw Lemmen's ambush face: rubbed over with black grease-crayon, boonie hat pulled down over his forehead. A moment later, in the dark again, Nuong heard Lemmen's ammo clip being pulled, then the metallic snaps of an unfolding cleaning rod, which rattled and scraped when he shoved it down the bore of his carbine. Nuong heard the rod being drawn out of the barrel, the rounds being taken out of the ammo clip one by one, being rubbed hard on the front of Lemmen's shirt, then going back into the clip, a click as each round found its place.

"What do you think, Sergeant Nuong?"

"I am trying not to think," Nuong said. "At least, I am trying not to think what is out there. It does no good. What is out there is out there. I was thinking about my son."

"How old is he?"

"Eleven."

"I didn't know he was that old," Lemmen said. "We are the same age, aren't we?"

"Yes, but we count it differently," Nuong said. "So I am older. I have a daughter, also," he said. "But I worry most about my son. Once I hoped he could go to school in America. That way, he would get out of this. But I could not afford to send him."

"How much would it take?" Lemmen asked.

"I have missed my chance," Nuong said.

Lemmen touched him with a pack of cigarettes. Nuong thought of turning it down, but needed a smoke for his nerves. He fumbled with the pack, put a cigarette in his mouth, drew his head back when the lighter flicked. He sucked in smoke. For some reason cigarettes, even American ones, were tasting foul. Perhaps he had smoked too many today. He took a final puff and threw the cigarette over the mud wall; it made an orange arc and landed with a hiss.

"My family would be out of this," Nuong said, "if I had acted like some others. Perhaps we are foolish to have faith in anything but ourselves."

Lemmen sucked on his cigarette and the glow showed black grease and a tight face.

"Forgive me for talking so much," Nuong said, "I am very worried about my family."

"I would take care of them," Lemmen said. "You could depend on that."

"Thank you," Nuong said. "Do you know where they are?"

Lemmen nodded, his cigarette moving up and down in the dark.

"I would do the same for you," Nuong said. "If you needed it."

"I have just about no family," Lemmen said. He smoked his cigarette and an orange glow escaped from his fingers; he was hiding it with both hands. "When you're in our army, you're always moving. In the States, most girls wouldn't give you a glance anyway—except whores on payday. Maybe."

"In our army it is no better," Nuong said. "Unless you are a man of rank. Then it is entirely different."

"Yes," Lemmen said. "The same in our army." He took a last puff of his cigarette; despite his careful hiding of it a moment before, he let it fall to the ground, where it threw off sparks. "Hoa Muon wants me to marry her and take her to the U.S."

"I am not surprised," Nuong said.

"What do you think of that idea?"

"She will make someone a good wife."

"What have I got to lose?" Lemmen said. "Except—I had this idea of retiring to her village. It is a beautiful spot."

"Sometimes," Nuong said. "But it is also backward. You would find that out if you lived there. Perhaps a compromise is called for. Perhaps you two would be happy in Saigon."

"It's a big, noisy city."

"Yes."

"I wanted to live along the Mekong. I've been dreaming about it for years. I used to be freezing, up in the mountains of Colorado, and I used to dream about it. Palm trees. The river. Boys fishing. Water buffalo. People keeping hogs and chickens. But I don't want to be a bachelor my whole life, Sergeant. I don't want to die and leave nothing behind."

"I understand."

Lemmen stuck out his hand. At first Nuong did not know why, but as he shook Lemmen's hand he heard behind him the scraping and shuffling of boots. A clinking sound also. "Well," Lemmen said, "here we go."

Lemmen watched the Arvins walk across the stick bridge one at a time, outlined in moonlight—small, skinny figures, like monkeys in helmets, balancing rifles. Once across, they disappeared. Except that once, in a lightning flash, Lemmen saw them clearly: they had formed a line, each soldier with an arm out holding on to the backpack in front of him, wading a waist-deep stream surrounded by reeds.

Nuong and Lemmen were last. Which puzzled Lemmen, since Nuong was supposed to interpret for the Dai-ui, who had crossed the bridge twenty soldiers ago. But Lemmen didn't have time to think about it. Nuong trotted over the bridge, holding his M-16 like a balancing stick; then he was lost in the darkness at the other side.

Lemmen's turn and he hesitated. The bridge was long and crooked—skinny tree limbs linked by rope, and supported by forked limbs sticking up from deep water. The bridge had bent even under the weight of Nuong.

Lemmen reached back and loosened the straps of his radio, then his pack. It crossed his mind that this was the

water from which Van had pulled those snakes; he can-
celed the thought, no use thinking now. He put one foot
on the bridge, let his weight down. Moved out a step. I can
do it, he told himself, it's like walking the rails back in
Rock Island. Forward! One foot in front of the other. The
limbs bent like a bow underneath him.

He put a shaky foot down near the first forked limb and
felt a shift. He stopped. He was sweating. He carefully
turned just his head to look backward. Too far along now
to lunge back for shore. He looked ahead, thought about
making a dash for it. Heard a ripple in the water. Ahead in
the darkness, Nuong called to him like an owl: "Woo-hoo."

Forward, he told himself. He went along, stopping for
balance, taking another step. The weight of his radio and
pack made every step shaky—he swerved and gyroed, the
pack and radio shifted and he had to fling himself backward, arms and hands going in crazy circles; he recovered.
In a flash of lightning he realized he'd be an easy target;
took quick steps, his rifle held out for balance, the
branches cracking—he tried to run, then crunch, he was
on his knees in mud, pieces of bridge all around him, rifle
held over his head.

Nuong was there, a skinny shadow in the dark; he held
his M-16 like a parallel bar and Lemmen slung his carbine
over his neck, grabbed on to Nuong's rifle, leveraged himself into a standing position. Ten pounds of mud clung to
him. He cinched the pack and radio tight on his back. Felt
for his ammo bandolier.

"Are you hurt?" Nuong whispered.

"I'm okay," Lemmen whispered. "This isn't a lucky beginning."

"We must hurry," Nuong whispered, and led as they
walked to catch up to the patrol. At first they walked in
mud that barely came over the soles of their boots. Soon it
was a few inches of water and, under that, ankle-deep
mud. It was impossible to put a foot down without making
a splash, or pick it up without mud sucking loudly at it. A

little farther into the swamp the water was over Lemmen's shins; soon it came over his knees, and they were wading down a stream.

Water came up to his nuts and Lemmen held his breath at the cold shock. Every step was a struggle. The pack and radio weighed heavier and heavier. The mud sucked at his boots with a slurping sound that Lemmen felt sure could be heard halfway to Cambodia.

He was breathing hard; he felt tired, heavy, and old. Every few steps he turned to check behind him. The compound wasn't far back, judging by the glow of those white tents—it seemed to be pulsing, faint one moment, dark the next. Or was he already seeing what wasn't there? Nuong seemed to be getting farther ahead. Lemmen wanted to throw his pack away; dismissed the thought. Unprofessional.

He followed Nuong and things closed in. He was surrounded by reeds in a narrow, winding stream of stinky water. The reeds were dark gray in the moonlight, dull green in the lightning flashes. They were high and he could put out a hand and touch a wall of them on either side. He had no vision except to the front, Nuong, and to the rear, darkness. The soldiers ahead made ripples, splashes, and loud sucking sounds when they pulled their boots out of the mud; Lemmen could hear the occasional spoken word, the clink of mess kits, nervous giggles, the clack of ammo bandoliers. All of that mixed with the thumping of his heart in his ears.

A prayer came up from somewhere and went through his mind: O my God, I am heartily sorry for having offended thee. And I detest all my sins because I dread the loss of heaven and the pains of hell. The rest of the prayer wouldn't come, but those words kept repeating on him. He tried to stop it. Tried to use reason on it—a prayer from grade school and here he needed to be sharp, alert, think tactics. What would he do if they made contact now? He tried to gain control of his thoughts.

He kept slogging, fighting to keep that prayer out of his brain; bizarre thoughts coming to him now, his father drunk and falling in the door on New Year's Eve, his mother walking him along shady streets to the bakery after mass, Holloway grinning with a Vietnamese girl on his lap, Carney's body faceup in a foot of muddy water, Buck Shannon revving his jeep—then something snapped, and he realized he was struggling along, a trooper, holding his rifle high away from the water. This is it, something told him—as if one part of his mind wanted a dialogue with the other. This could be the last thing I ever do. I could be the last man to die here. Let me be killed, he thought, but don't let me be captured.

He had lost sight of Nuong around a bend. He felt his skin pucker, his crotch tighten, his scalp and shoulder muscles harden. He knew something was about to go wrong. He kept looking into the reeds, then something made him look up to see a strange, real-seeming vision of Hoa. For a moment, a ghost of her seemed to be floating above him. She was neither angry nor happy, merely neutral and patient. Lemmen shook his head to get rid of the vision.

It would have made him insane, that hallucination, except that something like it had happened before—at the Seven Sisters. He later decided it was a kind of survival instinct, a splitting of the combat survivor from the normal human being. And this spooky, electric feeling—that, too, had been with him at the Seven Sisters. And kept him charged up and helped him make it!

His body kept tingling. He felt as if he were in two places at once. His lower self struggling through muck and water; his upper self floating above, watching calmly. Some third part of him knew the danger of coming apart and barked orders in his brain: Cavalry! Forward!

He slogged along. Things seemed brighter; reeds waved in the slightest breeze and the motion seemed evil somehow. A lightning flash went off, every muscle in his scalp knotted, he became afraid to look into the reeds ahead—a moment before he saw it, he knew it would be there, in all its unwordly brightness: the face of Charley, grinning, immortal, mocking him.

The patrol had been halted awhile before word came whispered down the line to Nuong and Lemmen. Lemmen knew what it would be, because the Arvins had started to settle in noisily. Nuong turned to him; his rifle clunked into the barrel of Lemmen's carbine, and he whispered: "Here."

At one side of the stream was a bank—mud and grass maybe a foot high, and the Arvins were putting rifles, mess kits, packs, and ammo on it, then hauling themselves, dark shapes, out of the water. Nuong, standing waist-deep in the stream, took his pack off, slung it on the bank, put his rifle in the crook of both arms, and elbowed and kneed his way up.

Lemmen got up on the rump too; it was thick, slippery mud, with high grass, not much wider than a sidewalk, but he was grateful for even semisolid ground. Still, he couldn't get completely out of the water, his legs dangling in the stream from below the knees. He worked his elbows into the mud. Moved himself up a few inches, parted the grass in front of him—its raspy edges cut his fingers, but he was intent on looking.

He had passed the state of visions, hallucinations, and trembling, and come to ice-cold reason and fear. They had made it to a good spot, and had settled in behind bullet-stopping mud, and when he looked through the grass it was with a tactician's eye. The lightning had mostly moved off, and the half-moon was the only light. At first it seemed all the same out there—wet and empty, reeds and water, black and gray. Then Lemmen began to see that the reeds made a snaky line fifty feet in front of them. He decided that the line of reeds marked the low-tide path Command had showed him from the helicopter. But there was no way to be sure. He worked the radio off his back, put it on his right side. Shed his pack, put his rifle on top of it, dug clips of wet ammo out of his bandolier.

He checked to his left, could see Nuong only in black outline. He looked through the grass again and thought the situation through: The enemy would come from the left, the west. There were thirty Arvin soldiers to Lemmen's left, but they were not to blow the ambush on their own. They were to wait for the Dai-ui to fire first. The idea was to avoid ambushing a unit until they knew how big it was. The absolute nightmare would be to ambush a VC squad scouting ahead of an NVA battalion. If the Dai-ui sensed that, they would call in to Hopkins and Tho, and try to sneak back into camp before the NVA found it.

But it wasn't ebb tide yet, Lemmen told himself, and Charley wasn't going to come down that stream until it dried up. With the landscape fixed, and the situation cast in his mind, Lemmen tried to relax. They can only come at low tide, he repeated to himself; they can only come from the left. He took off his boonie hat and put it in front of him. Swatted at mosquitoes buzzing his ears. Dug a Lucky out of his waterproof plastic pack, put it between his lips. Raw bite of tobacco. He put his hat back on, tightened the chin strap, let the cigarette dangle unlit from his lips. After a few minutes he dragged his field jacket out of his pack, laid it like a wet blanket between him and the mud. His lucky field jacket. A well-worn survivor of two tours: a hundred ambushes, fifty sweeps, forty fire missions, twenty convoys, any number of whorehouses and bars, thirty days of KP, a two-stripe bust in rank, one hot insertion at the Seven Sisters.

He wriggled around, settled himself in the mud and grass. Still couldn't bring his feet out of the water, resigned himself; he'd be wet all night. Feet and legs would be prunes by morning; the skin would disintegrate, he'd probably get an infection. Maybe that would be good for a medical profile. Maybe they'd send him to Saigon! He'd look up Worthington; in the last few years he'd run across him at Benning, at Ord, in Mannheim. But Worthington was never happy away from Vietnam, and he always had his transfer papers in. Maybe Worthington could find him an E-5 slot, a nice office job; Lemmen thought he could stand it in Saigon for a while.

He took his pop-flares out of his pack, shoved them in the sleeves of his jacket, hiding their aluminum glint. Took two grenades off his belt, straightened the ends of the cotter pins for an easy pull. Sweat ran down his face. More and more mosquitoes buzzed his ears. He swung at them a few times, shifted to one elbow, and watched through the grass, the carbine snug in his left arm. The Arvins were settled in now, and the noise was mostly swamp: insects and frogs, the buzzing of mosquitoes in his ears.

Lemmen stayed still, watched and waited, running all kinds of things through his mind. The loneliest job in the world, ambush. No contact at all with the man next to you; sometimes you couldn't even see his outline. For all the comfort they would give Lemmen in the next eight hours, Nuong and the others might as well be miles away. Unless, of course, they blew bush. I hope to God we don't blow bush, Lemmen thought. But no use thinking about it. Distraction, that's what was needed on ambush nights. Things to think about!

Hoa was the most pleasant thing he could think of. Lemmen wondered how he could get her safely to Saigon. The Delta was the nicest place he'd ever been: dreamy, hot, sleepy, and slow, all rice paddies and dirt roads, water buffalo and barefoot peasants. But if Saigon would be safer for a while, maybe he should see old Worthington. They could live nicely on Lemmen's pay—maybe Worthington could find a job for Hoa too. They could rent an apartment. It wouldn't be country living, though. He turned it over in his mind. Wasn't sure what he should do. Look up Worthington, that was the main thing. Maybe Worthington would have good advice on matters of love and war. Later they could come back to the Delta for the quiet, simple life. He watched the swamp. The Lucky in his mouth had disintegrated into bitter flecks; with silent puffs, he spit them out.

He watched, but there was hardly anything to see. Trying to keep your mind off the job, that was the trick. Thoughts drifting, from Hoa to Sharon and Sue; from Vinh Long to Saigon; from Fort Polk to Rock Island, then stopping on the day his mother died—she had been alone, that was his biggest regret. Lemmen was a private at Fort Polk, Louisiana, then. They called him out of formation one morning, and told him to report to the Red Cross. Running there, he knew already what the message would be. Stroke, a second and final one. He took a plane up to Rock Island and met an aunt and uncle who had driven up from Missouri and in three numb, miserable days, they settled everything. On the ride to the cemetery he remembered her squeezing orange juice, making him toast, packing his lunch for school; he remembered peeking out the bedroom door to see her smoking cigarettes, alone, and watching a late-night TV movie. He remembered her bundled in two bathrobes against the leaky cold of the

blue trailer they had in Illinois. Whenever his father criti-
cized him—*that report card is a disgrace . . . look at you, a
kid your size and you're afraid to go out for football . . . I had a
job when I was half your age*—his mother would come into
his room later and say: He doesn't mean those things, he
doesn't feel well—you just do your best. When he threw a
handful of dirt into her grave, that was it for his family.

Unless you counted the old man, and Lemmen sure
didn't. For as long as he could remember, the minute
things got difficult or unpleasant, the old man moved on.
Things were always too much for him: his boss was a rag-
ing maniac, or the pay was too low, or the work too hard,
or the winters too nasty or the summers too hot or the
neighbors too noisy or, the main excuse, he was wasting
his time in a place like this. Lemmen remembered Sun-
days in various towns, in a rented two-bedroom trailer,
the old man feeling guilty enough to stay home for a half
an afternoon, watching a TV football game, drinking his
beers, trying to explain the game to his son; if they were in
a state like Illinois, with the bars open on Sunday, he
might take a walk at halftime, and not come back until
long after dark. Lemmen did not expect the old man to
show up at his own wife's funeral; wasn't disappointed.

From the swamp there came an occasional ripple or
splash, snakes and rats coming out now that the soldiers
had been quiet awhile. Lemmen's thoughts drifted to Hoa
again. Back to the time he met her: at the Hello and Goodbye, which at that time had no name, just a sign that said
BAR OPEN. Lemmen, hot and sweaty from his first walking
tour of Vinh Long, sat in the darkest, coolest corner. A
skinny, pretty girl came to his table and said: We have cold
beer today. He looked her over. Sit down, he said, and
patted the space next to him. Thank you, Specialist, she
said, reading the rank off his collar. She sat down. How
did you learn to speak English? he asked.

I learn because I have a great desire to, she said. What
state are you from, Specialist—let me guess. California?

People who asked where he came from must have thought him a liar; what could he tell them but summers in Maine and Wisconsin, winters in Florida and New Mexico, springtimes in Charleston, autumns in Arkansas; he had attended fifteen schools in eleven states. His father was a gas attendant one month and a car salesman the next; then a cook, a janitor, a motel manager; he'd worked in factories that canned corn, assembled office furniture, mixed resins, stamped out auto parts, made window shades. Sixteen years of one town after another, and finally, in the Quad Cities, they moved into a real apartment, and his mother had said enough: Billy and I are staying. His father quit the furniture factory on the next payday and kept moving; his mother got a job in a department store. When he graduated from high school, Lemmen tried to make her happy for a while—as if to make up for the old man's neglect; he took a half semester of uninspiring junior college courses, told her he liked it, said maybe he would be a teacher, but somehow found himself beer-drunk, riding a Greyhound. When he woke up sober, in Colorado, it occurred to him, looking out at that rocky, cold landscape, that he was acting like the old man. But he couldn't go back; he was eighteen! So he stayed on the Hound another day and night, and at the California border he hit on a plan. He got off in Monterey and hitchhiked to Fort Ord. Ideas of discipline and purpose were running through his mind when a sergeant with a flattop haircut said: I can get you some good training, son, if you make a commitment to the six-year plan.

Past, present, and future, all jumbled, ran through his mind. For the future he saw a blank—at least until he could get up to visit Worthington. Or maybe Hopkins would assign him to Saigon, and he could bring Hoa. Then he'd really think marriage over. Did he love her enough? Or would he soon get tired of her—Saigon had whorehouses and bars that would tempt a saint. Would she be happy with Saigon or would she nag him about California? Only seven years to a pension—then they could live anywhere.

He envisioned himself retired on his rightful pension, a sergeant first class. He would talk Hoa out of her shameful obsession with the United States. Then, when things settled down, maybe he'd have one last week-long fling in the bars and whorehouses, marry Hoa, move back to the Delta; they would have beautiful golden slope-eyed children who would play happy, barefoot, and wild on the banks of the Mekong.

Mosquitoes—they were what brought him back to swamp reality. It was really their time of night; they were out for blood. What had been annoying squadrons of them became loud swarms, then buzzing clouds. They made so much noise in Lemmen's ears, he could no longer think or dream; they kept biting and diving and buzzing. Lemmen tried to fend them off by waving his arms and hands but it was hopeless; soon they got so thick he couldn't breathe without sucking them in. Desperate, he made a mask out of a damp handkerchief, tied it across his nose and mouth, breathed through it. Then he closed his eyes against them. Finally he put down his carbine and covered his ears with his hands.

A long, long time passed like that, the kind of time that can't be measured, like time in pain. Mosquitoes bit him everywhere: face, hands, wrists, and neck, they bit through his uniform, got into his boots to bite his ankles. He itched all over from bites and from swamp water, the uniform drying like an extra, filthy layer of skin. After a while he had to open his eyes; he kept the mosquitoes out by constant blinking. Then he gave up, took his hands from his ears, and let the mosquitoes fly in. Rolled over quietly and scratched himself against the grass like a dog. Lay there awhile, his carbine across his chest, looking at the moon through a net of flying insects.

From his left came restless Arvin movements: splashes, slaps, whispered cursing. We'll be lucky, Lemmen told himself, if they don't hear us in Cambodia. The Arvins were probably near mutiny. He took a wristwatch out of his top pocket. Was that all? Maybe it had stopped. Yes. He shook it. Looked again. The glowing dot of the second hand stayed still. Watch was supposedly waterproof. Typical PX watch. He shook it again. Doesn't matter, he told himself, and pocketed the watch. We're here until daylight anyway.

He rolled over on his stomach. Looked over the swamp, then closed his eyes for a while. One sip, he told himself. Opened his eyes. Scanned the swamp. Got the bourbon bottle out of his side pocket. Put the bottle and his canteen in front of him. Sipped from the bottle, sipped from the canteen. Then got an idea. He put bourbon in his hand like after-shave, spread it over his face. It stung good in the mosquito bites. Bourbon on his ears and neck. The mosquitoes still buzzed in clouds but weren't landing on his skin. Lemmen congratulated himself with another sip. But discipline, discipline. He capped the bottle, slid it into his pocket. He lay there, his left hand on Sam, and seemed to doze off for a while.

Sergeant Nuong caught a whiff of bourbon, and later heard a snort that could have been a snore, or could have been a frog. He was fairly sure it was Lemmen, sleeping. His first thought was to crawl over and touch Lemmen on the shoulder, to stop him from snoring. But before he could move he was startled by the sound of metal clanking. Three times. Rhythmic and loud.

He flattened himself, put his M-16 on the hump, and stared out. There was nothing to see, except that the tide had run out, and the stream had nearly become a path. He listened hard, but heard only the natural sounds of the swamp.

He reached for his canteen. A sip of water might put him back in contact with reality. Because surely he couldn't have heard a loud, bell-like sound, couldn't have heard it three times; no one would dare make such a sound, and even if someone did, it would have caused shooting up and down the line. Fear and night brought strange things, and not only to the eyes. Nuong lifted his canteen to his lips.

But the water turned copper-tasting in his mouth when he heard the noise again—clang, clang, clang—and he dropped his canteen and put his finger on the trigger of his rifle. The hair on his body went erect, his skin puckered, his muscles twitched, his balls drew into his body. To his left he heard a splash, a rustle. He backed into the water, stood, keeping the mud bank in front of him, and turned toward the noise with his rifle.

He heard something at his back and whipped around—his rifle was pointed at Lemmen's face. Lemmen, with one hand, slowly pushed the rifle barrel aside, then put his finger to his lips. He stooped to Nuong's height. Both of them in water to their knees.

"What's going on?" Lemmen whispered.

Nuong shook his head. He twisted his body, made a two-finger beckon. He lifted his foot out of the mucky bottom in slow-motion silence. Moved his leg carefully through the water, making no splash; put his foot down again, inches ahead. Took another careful step. Froze for a moment when Lemmen, behind him, made a ripple.

He waited for silence, then started again, slowly pulling his back foot out. It made a sucking sound, and once again he stopped to listen. Insects and frogs. They were quiet, though, and distant, as if the creatures nearby had been frightened into silence. Nuong stayed still. Patience. He figured the nearest Arvin private to be ten or fifteen feet away. He pursed his lips to sound the birdlike Arvin password, but his mouth and throat were too dry. He licked his lips but that was no help; his tongue felt swollen. He took another slow, careful step, his M-16 jammed into his shoulder and pointed forward.

From up the line came a tiny clink, and that set off a panic of loud clanking that lasted five full seconds, and Nuong dropped into a crouch. When the noise stopped, there was a moment of pure silence before the insects started up again. In that silence Nuong realized that the

Arvins were deliberately clanging their pots and pans. But why?

Nuong turned to see if Lemmen was still behind, and as he did so, felt Lemmen's big hand on his shoulder.

"Dai-ui," Lemmen whispered, and pointed forward, and Nuong nodded and rose from his crouch.

He moved out toward midstream, so as not to scare any Arvins by coming too close. He waded faster now, the muck sucking at his boots, the water slurping and rippling. He passed quickly behind the soldiers, hardly seeing them on the dark and muddy rump they clung to.

He stopped when he saw the antenna. He whispered, "Dai-ui Loan," and managed to make a half note of birdlike sound. He waded past the legs and boots of the Dai-ui's lieutenants, who were prone on the bank, rifles pointed out. A few more mud-sucking steps and Nuong saw, in dark grays, the Dai-ui himself, sitting cross-legged in mud, soft glow of the radio dial between his legs, his back to the swamp.

Nuong dropped into a squat. Why are we making such noise? he asked.

Why are you asking me? the Dai-ui said. What are these crazy men doing? They are scaring the shit out of me. The Dai-ui grinned, whether from nervousness or something else, Nuong could not tell. In that grin, there was a sparkle of gold teeth, and then, in a glimmer of lighting, Nuong saw the Dai-ui's full face, and his cavalry hat outlined against the sky. His face was stiff and full of fear.

What will I tell the American sergeant? Nuong asked.

Tell him anything you like, the Dai-ui said. But if this racket keeps up, there is no way I'm staying out here.

Nuong stood and turned around, with a good idea of what was happening. He motioned to Lemmen to bend forward, then whispered at his ear. "He is ready to break the ambush."

"Fine with me," Lemmen said. "What's the deal?"

"He does not know himself," Nuong said. "He is very

frightened—they are rebelling on him, with their pots and pans."

Lemmen looked past Nuong at the Dai-ui, then down at Nuong again. "They're rebelling? Or is he in on it?"

Be quiet, the Dai-ui said. He started talking into the radio, calling for headquarters. He whispered his call sign twice, waited through static, then told Nuong: Get back into position. I'll pass the word if they let us break the ambush.

Nuong put his finger to his lips, signaled for Lemmen to back away. Lemmen moved a few steps, and Nuong slipped in front, led them downstream to their places on the bank. Nuong lay his rifle there, crawled up; slimy cold mud went down his shirt. Lemmen came out of the water slipping and splashing.

"If they keep making noise, Charley will find us," Lemmen said in a whisper.

"The Dai-ui knows this," Nuong whispered. "He is calling Colonel Tho now. And Colonel Tho will call your major."

"What the hell's he going to tell them?"

"The Dai-ui? He will lie, of course," Nuong whispered. Lemmen touched him with something hard: a bottle. Nuong took it, held it to the sky, bourbon, half full. He uncapped the bottle, smelled it, brought it to his lips for a mouthful. The warm liquor on his tongue made him realize how cold and wet he felt. He capped the bottle and handed it back into the dark space that was Lemmen. He shivered, a chill shooting along his spine and shoulders; it shuddered and shook him.

"The Dai-ui cannot stop them, and perhaps does not want to," Nuong whispered.

Lemmen handed him the bottle again.

"We should be quiet if we can," Nuong said. He drank, and gave Lemmen the bottle back. It was silent for a while, and Nuong stared into the darkness, trying to get some idea of what, if anything, was out there; but a distant lightning flash ruined his night vision. All he could see for a while was formless black-and-gray. He shut his eyes to hurry his night vision back. He listened.

It was quiet for only a minute, then came a *ping* from up the line; then a pot thumping, a pan banging, and suddenly there was clanging everywhere, then one tiny M-16 pop—then an explosion of gunfire in red tracers, and Nuong pulled hard on the trigger, the rifle stuttering in his hands, brass hissing as it hit the water around him—in seconds, he was out of ammo and there was a lull, a few pops here and there, and Nuong lifted his head to reach for his bandolier, heard the fizz of pop-flares going up; a quick look in front of him showed an empty path under bright drifting light. A rifle popped off somewhere. From out of the darkness came the shouts of many soldiers: cease-fire.

Little America

Daylight, the helicopter revving to takeoff speed, Lemmen inside, the rotor noise seeming to beat against his eardrums. He had backed away from the argument. Which was between the crew chief and the Dai-ui, Nuong in the middle. The crew chief and the Dai-ui were screaming. Lemmen backed into the canvas seat, cinched the strap over his belly, breathed out hard.

The Dai-ui held his cavalry hat on his head, the prop wash blowing at it. He put one hand on the door pole, as if to hoist himself in, and the visor-faced crew chief put his foot on the Dai-ui's chest, pushed him back. The ship jiggled as if to rise. With one hand, the Dai-ui hung on to the pole. He screamed something lost in the noise. The crew chief pushed Nuong out of the way and his boot nudged the Dai-ui's hand. The Dai-ui wouldn't let go of the pole, the crew chief drew his boot back, kicked the Dai-ui's hand, hard, there was blood, the Dai-ui still wouldn't let go, the crew chief's boot gave him a vicious kick to the face, the air was all bloody droplets, the helicopter rose and left the Dai-ui sitting in the mud, holding his face in both hands, cavalry hat blowing away.

The Dai-ui was ten feet, fifty feet, a hundred feet down. Except for Lemmen and Nuong, the chopper was empty. Nuong buckled a red safety strap across his chest; he had dropped his muddy rifle, backpack, and ammo bandolier among Lemmen's things on the steel floor. Overhead was a turning shaft; in the metalwork walls were wires and tubing. Lemmen stared at those mechanical things, couldn't look out the door. Nuong was bent almost double in the canvas seat, his uniform stiff with mud from boots to collar, his face puffy with mosquito bites, mud in his crew-cut hair. Nuong untied his boots, stripped off his crusty socks, kicked them under his seat. His feet were an ugly black-and-purple.

Lemmen found himself looking at his own boots, the leather and canvas thick with gray mud. He started thinking over the questions he wanted to ask Nuong about last night; but any talk would be lost in the roar and pop. He looked up to see the back of the crew chief's helmet, the chief angling his doorgun down at the fort, ready to fire, and a horrible thought occurred to Lemmen—was the Dai-ui shooting at them? He twisted in his seat to look out.

But the helicopter was banking and he couldn't see the Dai-ui. He caught a glimpse of the two mortars, the piles of ammo crates they'd left there, and thought he saw Van, by himself near the mortars, waving. The chopper banked harder and Lemmen lost sight of Post Twelve, he could only see blue sky out one door and swamp out the other, and when they were level again, Post Twelve had almost disappeared.

No, Lemmen thought, the Dai-ui wouldn't dare fire, the crew chief was just taking no chances. He thought about Van—in the confusion and rush of things, they had never made him give back the radio. Let him keep it! What a miserable life to live, out there with snakes and mosquitoes—and the Dai-ui for a father! What would the

NVA do to women and children? Of course they would spare them, he told himself. He tried to cultivate pleasant thoughts. Conjured a memory of Hoa. There was a trick he liked to play on her. In the days when the Hello and Goodbye was crowded with GIs, he would come up behind her, cover her face with his hands, and say: VC. You pay rice tax. Don't play, Hoa would say, and twist away from him. She got angry in a flash, that girl. She reminded him of a much skinnier Sophia Loren. The Vietnamese: the Italians of the Orient.

He remembered when they'd made love, when they'd gotten drunk in her room while listening to the radio, and one really good time when they'd packed a picnic lunch, rice cakes and cold fish, and Hoa took him to a swimming cove on the Mekong. Lemmen got lost remembering that, and when he found himself in the present again, he looked down; they were flying over rice paddies, all bright green, and striped with brown canals. Civilization! The paddies square, the canals straight. Hundreds of miles of canals, thousands of miles of dikes, all dug by hand over the centuries. As much an accomplishment as the Pyramids. The patience! The faith! And people said there was no optimism in the Orient. Lemmen had seen those diggers once, down near Can Tho, knee-deep in water, wearing conical hats, raking muck with wooden hoes. He'd thought: I could be watching a scene from a thousand years ago.

He found himself staring at Nuong's black-and-purple feet. Which made him feel sick and cold because that was the color of Jimmy Carney when they took him out of the Mekong. Lemmen remembered that streak of ugly luck that started with Holloway at the Seven Sisters and kept going until the day they found Carney, bloated, not human anymore, just a black-and-purple log floating in the Mekong.

Holloway was a newbie, a black kid from Flint, Michigan, chubby, with a quick, easy smile. Down at the Hello and Goodbye, the girls named him Billboard because of a billboard ad that dominated Vinh Long's traffic circle. The ad was for Hynos toothpaste, and showed a middle-aged African man with a dazzling smile, a smile something like Holloway's. So those were Holloway's names: to his family he was Earl, to the squad he was Newbie, to the bar girls he was Billboard. Lemmen liked the guy; he was careful, and had the right amount of fear, he wasn't trying to prove how brave he was; sensible, for nineteen. Lemmen thought he would be a top trooper; all he needed was to take a little fire and learn he could survive it.

Lemmen had been at Delta Town for a few months when Holloway came—it was hard to remember time exactly; the day seemed to be the only unit of measure; weeks and months and seasons had no meaning. But sometime not much before Lemmen had arrived in the Delta, Charley had overrun the base for the one-night victory in which he lost Vinh Long province for years. When Lemmen had arrived, the moldy wooden barracks of Delta Town were still stuck with thousands of fléchette arrows, from the explosion Charley had set off at the ammo dump.

Back then there was another Command, Major Manning, and he was furious about being overrun, he had lost an officer friend and his top sergeant, and wanted revenge. Some time after Holloway arrived, Intelligence finally heard that the VC who had overrun the base were hiding in caves in the Seven Sisters. Intelligence as usual was half right.

The 9th Cav went in at dusk, in choppers, all that noise, all those aviation lights, Lemmen's squad first. They jumped out behind heavy bush at the base of a slope and the chopper had barely lifted off when the darkness erupted in bright green tracers and tremendous noise, and everybody got down in tall grass, all separated, all lost, hugging dirt while Manning, in the sky, ordered the chopper to circle and pick them up again, all the choppers pouring down fire wildly, Bumstead and Carney crawling screaming through the weeds, dragging something that turned out to be Holloway.

Mission aborted, nothing accomplished, and minutes later they were high and away from it, inside a chopper, the only light was the orange pinpoints of cigarettes, and in the darkness between them, the gurgling, dying Holloway.

Nobody ever seemed sure after that. Nobody really knew what killed Holloway—maybe cav helicopter machine guns, maybe NVA gunners, maybe both. Nobody was sure why Manning had fallen for the VC's sucker tactics—the hills were full of NVA machine guns. Nobody knew why they had to charge in like the old-time cavalry. Nobody could figure out why or even if chasing the VC was important. The day after Lemmen and Bumstead drove Holloway's bagged body to graves registration, the *Stars and Stripes* started running stories about American troop withdrawals.

It haunted Lemmen, sometimes, that the guys in his old squad, draftees like Bumstead and Little, with their defeatist attitudes, might have been right. What, after all, had they accomplished in this country? What made it worth Holloway, Carney, Buck Shannon—or even the life of that VC scout out in the swamp?

Which brought his mind around to Buck. He was everybody's pal. The thing Buck loved to do was drive convoy. They would get in gun jeeps and escort truckloads of food and ammo down to the Arvins at Rach Jia, and Buck always took point, driving hard. He would stop for nothing, he always said, but a cold beer. His theory of convoy driving was speed: By the time Charley knows I'm coming, I'll be already gone. That's why they called him Buck, because of how he drove the jeep. Buckaroo.

Then on just another convoy to Rach Jia, Buck swerved his jeep around a cyclo, he must have had a six-pack in him. The jeep flipped over, Buck under it with a broken

neck. Lemmen wasn't there, but the guys who saw it remembered how the jeep wheels kept spinning.

Lemmen wrote the condolence letter. What good would
the truth do? So he wrote lies to some people he'd never
met, Mr. and Mrs. William Shannon, he could only imagine them, living in a trim house in Pennsylvania, blue hills
all around, their garden just coming up, when an official
army car pulls into the driveway.

Lemmen worked on that letter like nothing else in his
life. Ripping up draft after draft. Describing Buck's hero-
ism in glowing terms and not much detail. How Buck was
killed while trying to maneuver his jeep into position during an enemy ambush. How he died trying to save the
truck drivers and his buddies. Died doing his duty. Died
so others might live. All that crap. Lemmen wouldn't type
it, too impersonal. He put it down in his neatest, most
sober handwriting. Then he persuaded Manning to break
loose with a bronze star; Lemmen folded the stiff citation
in with the letter, sealed the envelope, walked it to the
Delta Town post office, dropped it in the slot, and that's
when he really knew it: the clink of that mailbox door was
the eulogy, and Buck Shannon of Shippensburg, Pennsylvania, was gone.

Lemmen looked down and they were flying over a highway, sluggish traffic, all of it going to Saigon, nothing
coming back to the Delta. The traffic was mostly olive-
drab vehicles and cyclos, jammed to a crawl on a rusty
bridge that crossed a wide river. Huge chain-link fences
were the rails of the bridge—rocket screens.

He put a Lucky in his mouth and lit it. Breathed out
smoke that was sucked away by the prop wash. When he
first came over here, he expected soldiers to die charging
machine guns, rifles blazing, hand grenades flying—like
movie heroes, all glory. But he had never, in two tours,
seen or even heard of anything heroic, glamorous, or glori-
ous. Instead he saw the boys—they were only boys!—die
in jeeps, in whorehouses, in barroom brawls; of food

poisoning, drug overdoses, helicopter crashes; they drowned, they walked backward into booby traps, they were shot by snipers nobody saw. Look at his own squad. Holloway died twitching two thousand feet over a worthless swamp—all for the revenge of some major who right now was probably drinking a Scotch and water in some stateside club, and didn't even remember Holloway's name. Buck went down to simple drunken driving. Carney, loaded on skag, just walked into the Mekong. In all of it, the dark shadow of self-destruction.

He should have known, at least about Carney. When Carney switched from Chesterfields to Salems, that should have been enough for Lemmen right there. Of course. Salems with the first quarter inch of tobacco tapped out, and purple heroin packed in. The menthol made it easier to choke down the bitter smoke. But Lemmen didn't know that then, didn't suspect anything until Carney started sleeping fourteen hours a day, missing duty here and there —by the time Lemmen was ready to send him to the medics, he had vanished from his bed, and turned up two days later a purple log.

The end of another senseless mission, and these were thoughts he had after every one of them. Lemmen shook his head. New things coming, he told himself—couple of days of fun, then a new assignment. It would be great to see Worthington again and get drunk with him. Hadn't seen that old bastard since Ord. Lemmen looked out the door and they were high over another wide river, but this one ran through a city. Big city. Docks and cranes and ships lining the river. Looking north, Lemmen saw a cluster of sparkling whitish-green high-rises, and a flatter, rust-red and smoke-gray city spread around them. Two days off. Something in him started to rise. He could see Tan Son Nhut, no mistaking that big gray airport, dug into bright red earth. Beyond it an olive-drab sprawl: Little America.

From his seat in the cafeteria Sergeant Nuong had a view out the green-tinted picture window: a paved main street, down which, every few minutes, drove a jeep or truck filled with Americans. They were dressed not in jungle fatigues but in the khaki uniforms of office soldiers, or the thin white shirts of civilians. They were going home. The phrase echoed in Nuong's mind. He looked at the cafeteria clock—fifteen minutes after twelve; Lemmen was late.

He played with a Coca-Cola bottle, swishing the last ounce of brown liquid. On his meal tray were the stripped bones of fried chicken, and untouched string beans and mashed potatoes, all in compartments. Nuong drank the last of the Coca-Cola and stared out the window. What he saw was not the big supermarket–department store, not the massage parlor, not the movie theater, not the two-story office buildings with their wide, neat lawns. What he envisioned was his wife, son, and daughter being lifted in a canvas strap to the deck of a fishing boat. That vision lasted hardly a second, then Nuong found himself staring into dark green glass. The window was the exact color of the visors of helicopter crewmen. Which reminded Nuong of the nasty thing that happened just that morning, when the Dai-ui was kicked in the face. It was perhaps justified, that kick in the face, but remembering it made Nuong angry—and nervous. Somehow it made him nervous for his family.

He must have been very distracted because Lemmen surprised him by tapping on the window. Lemmen was outside, beckoning. Except for a can of beer, he was empty-handed. What has gone wrong? Nuong asked himself as he pushed back his chair and walked, trying not to seem anxious, toward the door. He pushed it open and was immediately transported from a cool room that smelled of fried chicken and disinfectant to hot air stinking of garbage and bad water.

"I'm a little drunk," Lemmen said. "Stopped at the club. Come on." His face was full of sweat, his uniform heavy with it. He was still in muddy jungle fatigues.

Nuong followed him—how could Lemmen walk so fast in this heat? They went across the main street, it was bubbling like fresh tar. They walked along a sidewalk, then up steps, through the gate of a fence, and onto the shimmering hot concrete around a swimming pool. The pool was filled with American men—old ones, young ones, black ones, white ones—jumping to hit a ball back and forth over a net, a game Nuong hadn't seen before. Lemmen finished the beer, crushed the can casually in one hand, tossed the flattened thing at a trash can, and said, "Two points," when it went in. Nuong did not understand exactly what he meant.

"Don't worry," Lemmen told him. "I've taken care of everything, you'll see." He led Nuong into the cool shade of a locker room. Nuong kept looking over his shoulder at the GI water game.

"I cannot help but thinking," Nuong said. "They do not know what we know."

"What are you saying?" Lemmen asked. From his

pocket he took a key attached to a square of red metal. He squatted and opened one of the lockers.

"If they knew what was happening, they would be as frightened as I am."

In the bottom of the locker was Lemmen's backpack, still encrusted with swamp mud. But now it was bulging and strapped tight. "I damn near bought them out," Lemmen said. He took a blue card out of his top pocket; it was punched full of holes; he let it flutter to the ground. "Used my whole ration card."

Nuong nodded; it was good of Lemmen to do him this favor without asking questions. Lemmen took off his shirt, the dark hair on his chest all wet with sweat. He sat on a wooden bench and untied his combat boots, kicked them off, groaned as he pulled off his muddy socks. He dropped the shirt, boot, and socks into a wire basket, then sat, breathing hard, as if he had to recover from the effort. "I can't invite you in for a swim," he said. "But I know you've got things to do anyway."

"We may not see each other after this," Nuong said. "Of that I am fairly certain."

"We ought to go have a drink," Lemmen said.

"I cannot right now," Nuong said.

"Want to meet me tonight in town, have dinner?"

"I have very busy plans."

"Well, maybe if I get assigned up here . . ."

"Yes, perhaps," Nuong said. "Sergeant Lemmen, you are not afraid now?"

Lemmen looked at him. "I don't know what to think," he said. "Little America's still open, and Saigon's still there, B-52s are flying—hard to believe it's all going to change in the blink of an eye."

"Yes," Nuong said. "Hard to believe."

"You'd better take that pack while I'm here," Lemmen said. He pointed to it. "Otherwise . . ."

"Yes," Nuong said. He knew what Lemmen had left

unsaid: Otherwise, they will think you are the pool boy, stealing. He squatted, drew the pack out of the locker, slipped it on, stood, cinched it around his shoulders. It was heavy and not well packed. He could feel the edges of cigarette cartons against his back, hear the clink of liquor bottles.

"Hitch a ride out," Lemmen said. "Don't try to walk past the gate. If you're riding, the guards won't check you."

"Thank you, Sergeant Lemmen."

"I know I'll see you around, Sergeant Nuong." They were shaking hands. Then Nuong backed to the door and gave Lemmen a salute, and walked along the pool fence.

The Americans were jumping and shouting in their water game. There were short lines of soldiers at the tiny tin huts selling hamburgers and pizza, and a long line of them waited for ice cream. To the left of the pool was the PX, a giant thing; atop its glaring tin roof an American flag drooped as if tired of the heat. Beyond, and downhill, was a stretch of the older, darker barracks—except for this main street, Little America belonged to the Arvins now. Encircling the whole base was a narrow dirt road, then a wide swath of barbed wire, and tall towers, and there it looked once again like a war zone.

He stood at the pool fence; felt unable to say goodbye. Little America reminded him so much of the United States, and he remembered his time there fondly. In California he'd been given eight weeks of mortar and infantry tactics, a year of language classes, and six months of special duty, during which his only job was to meet Americans and perfect his English.

California had filled his mind with images he might never shake: supermarkets the size of airports, restaurants that had no limit to eating, color television around the clock, highways and automobiles without end, ordinary people living in health and peace and plenty. What had the Big People done to please God? He stared past the splashing GIs, remembering: Not many years ago, when the Americans first came to build Little America, it was hardly the size of a city block, and it looked Vietnamese—muddy tents along crooked streets. A few years later it had been built up to block after block of barracks, with a paved road; next year there was a helicopter landing strip, a hospital, a huge bar-casino; the perimeter was lit with floodlights, planted with electronic sensors. Then for three straight years it expanded still more, dark-green earthmovers plowing huge tracts of red dirt until Little America was its own city.

Nuong often wondered why these big, rich people had sent their sons to die in his little nothing of a faraway country, and after two years in America and much asking, and much thought, he decided that Americans themselves had no idea. They did not know why they came, so naturally they did not know why they were leaving. Sometimes Nuong wished they had never come at all. Did they know what they were doing, leaving people with only the Arvin?

The Arvin. Army of the Republic of Vietnam—even the words were a shameful joke. What army? What republic? What Vietnam? The Big People did not understand that Vietnamese boys were forced to pick up a rifle, put on a uniform—take a chance with the VC, or take a chance with the Americans—only two ways to survive. The Big People dreamed the idea that the Arvin was an army—but to have a real army you must first have a real nation. Once the Big People left entirely, the Arvin would fight on in panic for a while, then collapse, Nuong was more sure of that than ever—how could he forget the sound of pots and pans?

"Sergeant Nuong!" It was Lemmen. Calling to him from the pool. Lemmen in water to his shoulders, his arms out on the edges of the pool. Hair heavy with water. He drew himself out of the pool, walked over, dripping, pulling up his green boxer trunks. Nuong stood in his shadow.

"You had the strangest look on your face," Lemmen said.

"I was only thinking," Nuong said.

On a stage over the bar, four dark girls in hiked-up white skirts sang "Help Me Make It Through the Night." Badly. In their mouths the words sounded something like *Hap Me May It Droo Ta Nie.* Three of the girls banged guitar chords; the other girl bashed drums out of time. The worst music Lemmen had ever heard. He was getting hornier by the minute.

He was drinking maybe his sixth bourbon. Who could count? What beautiful girls. He had it figured out: They were from Guam or the Philippines. Lemmen wanted it to be the Philippines. Which was far superior to Guam, having more single women, better weather, and truly foreign prices. A lot of old sergeants retired to the Philippines. Good raunchy place to settle down.

He swirled his bourbon, looked into it. Golden liquor ran down the sides of his glass, into a dark, dreamy pool. At his right hand, an ashtray was full of spent Luckies. God, did he want to get laid—he owed himself; a delayed celebration of his birthday. He could have caught a ride to Tu Do Street hours ago, and tried to find that Saron and

Shu—Sharon and Sue!—but no, he'd wasted the afternoon trying to look up Worthington, with no luck except that some guy at the mess hall said he'd heard that Worthington was in Saigon. That was at dinner, too late to go searching strange parts of the city, so Lemmen had come here, to the man's favorite haunt. Maybe he'd show up. Worthington had probably downed more drinks in this casino-bar than any man dead or alive.

Lemmen was getting lonely for Hoa. He wished he could just go to the phone and call her. Tell her to wait up, he'd catch the next bus and come down, they could make love and drink and talk. For once Lemmen longed for a few American conveniences: a Greyhound cruising a smooth highway at night; a telephone with the soft, sleepy voice of his girl at the other end; an all-night diner with strong coffee. He took a drink of bourbon. The girl singers looked better than ever. Their skin like Hershey bars. Their eyes like almonds. Their lips, cherries. Their tits, bouncing plums. Lemmen, a starving man!

He was fooling himself with these thoughts of Hoa. He'd never be able to stay with one woman. He wanted every woman he ever saw, that was the problem. One part of him wanted to marry Hoa but a bigger, more powerful part wanted to roam the raunchy edges of army bases for discount booze and payday romance. Drink and strange women, that was his problem and he finally admitted it. Which made him think about his father—place to place, town to town—what devils pushed that man on? Suddenly, Lemmen wished he knew the old man's address, so he could write. But what exactly would he say?

Someone tapped him on the back—Nuong! He was dressed in civilian clothes: baggy pants and a shiny beige shirt, a brown stripe on the pocket; he wore a gold Seiko watch, too big for his wrist, on the thick of his forearm. Nuong the civilian! Behind him, and out of focus, a few khaki GIs played their choice of the hundreds of slot machines in a huge, half-lit cavern.

"You cannot be rid of me so easily," Nuong said.

"Sit down," Lemmen said. "Have a drink."

Nuong stood, although there were plenty of stools. At one time this bar would have been five-deep, mostly with kids, in jungle fatigues, screaming for nickels and beer. Now the GIs were older, dressed in khakis, outnumbered by empty chairs and stools.

"Boy-san," Lemmen shouted over the music. The bar boy turned Lemmen's way; he was maybe four feet tall. "Budweiser and one of these." Lemmen held up his glass. He looked at Nuong. "I see you made it home," he shouted. "How is your son?"

"Well," Nuong said.

Lemmen nodded. The bar boy brought the drinks and Nuong picked up his sweating bottle and sipped.

"Your wife and daughter?" Lemmen shouted. The band finished its song and Lemmen's words hung, too loud, in the smoky air.

"Well," Nuong said, without looking at Lemmen. "I am thinking I will cross the line."

"What?"

"I must talk seriously with you, Sergeant Lemmen. I need to know if you have plans for escaping."

"Escaping?" Lemmen said. The girls in the band struck a loud, fast, awful "Proud Mary," and Lemmen took a second to think, to look at the girls, before shouting an answer.

"I'm not thinking of escaping," he said. He took a hit from his cigarette and shifted his eyes to the girl singers. He wanted to hold on to the dream of the good life that might be his: Guam, Hawaii, the Philippines.

"I've been sitting here thinking all afternoon . . ." Lemmen said, then stopped, regrouped. Waited through a clash of cymbals and a shouted chorus.

Lo-deen . . .
Okay

Lo-deen . . .
Okay
Lo-deen on a libber

"It is so loud," Nuong shouted. "How do you take it on your ears?"

"Old mortarman," Lemmen yelled. "Blown eardrums. Let's drink up and take a walk." He pointed at the beer bottle. "They won't let you take it outside." Nuong left his beer on the bar and stood back; Lemmen downed his drink. Nuong first, they walked past pool tables with only the cue balls up, down an aisle of blinking slot machines. At the last machine, Nuong stopped and searched his pockets, then Lemmen gave him a nickel. Nuong put the coin in, bit his lower lip, and pulled the handle: lemon, melon, plum. "I did not think so," he said.

"Want to get some more nickels and play?" Lemmen asked.

Nuong shook his head.

Outside it was dark and damp; the door closed on all but a faint echo of "Proud Mary." Lemmen lit a Lucky and started them walking toward the arc lights of the perimeter. Out on the night horizon were the popping flares of a Cobra trying to find the enemy, an occasional distant thud or red burst of tracers. They walked halfway down the block before Lemmen knew what he wanted to say: "I was sitting there thinking: Here I am a year older, it won't be that long until I'm retired. I'm getting a little too old to spend my life in bars and whorehouses, don't you think, Nuong?"

Nuong said nothing; he stared out at the horizon.

"But I can't see myself dragging Hoa from one army post to the next. In the States, I'm a nobody—you understand that, don't you, Nuong? I think I've finally made up my mind. I'm going to try to get permanent duty in Saigon, and bring her up with me."

"Perhaps you should transfer to the States," Nuong said.

"I really want to stay here."

"Myself no less!" Nuong said. "But I am leaving all the same."

That stopped Lemmen and all he could do in reply was look at Nuong. "What did you mean back there when you said 'escaping'?"

"I told you, I am crossing the line. You must know why. You were there, too, Sergeant."

"But up here it's the First Division, Nuong. They're topnotch."

"It is more dangerous here every day, I am convinced."

"By what?" Lemmen said. "By rumors? There's a new rumor every day. I heard a rumor this morning that the air force was ready to nuke Hanoi." Lemmen saw a shine of arc lights reflected in Nuong's hard, wet brown eyes. Nuong's left eye seemed to have lost its filmy look.

"You think my country will step back and do nothing?" Lemmen said. "After everything that's happened over here?" He flicked the cigarette away.

They began walking again, Nuong behind. At the perimeter road Lemmen stopped and looked out: guard towers, arc lights, sandbag bunkers, rolls of concertina wire, barbed-wire fences, a grassy minefield, all lit like a baseball stadium. Lemmen put his hands in his trouser pockets. Breathed in. Watched the horizon as a Cobra dived and let out a neon stream of Minigun fire.

"I am very pleased for the chance to come up and visit my family," Nuong said. "For me it is rare. Will you thank the major for me? Please tell him I do not mean to be rude." Lemmen nodded. He understood that Nuong was beginning to say goodbye.

"I must ask you for another favor," Nuong said. He paused; somewhere off in the dark, closer, was a short burst of automatic gunfire.

"Go ahead," Lemmen said.

"I am a bit embarrassed."

"Please ask me."

"You are free, of course, to say no."

Lemmen waited.

"There are boat captains waiting off Vung Tau, and every day their price is going up. Today their price went up to a hundred and twenty in American."

"How much do you need?"

"I made a hundred dollars this afternoon, and with my savings, I need forty-five more. I am offering this . . ." He took off his watch; from his pocket he got a gold chain and crucifix, held them out. "You may take these in exchange."

"I don't want them," Lemmen said. Took out his wallet and counted: Twenty, forty, forty-five, fifty, fifty-two. "This is what I have. Take it. I can get more."

"Now you take this," Nuong said, and held out the watch and chain.

"No," Lemmen said.

"Yes, they will steal it from me anyway."

"Who?"

"The boatmen."

Lemmen sighed. He took the watch on two fingers and jammed it down his hip pocket; dropped the chain into one of the pouches of his billfold. Nuong folded the dollar bills, kept them in his fist. "I hope to see you someday, Sergeant," Nuong said. "Perhaps I will buy back my watch and chain."

"I'll keep it for you," Lemmen said, then embraced Nuong, a quick hug in which the little sergeant seemed like the wispiest thing in the world.

Hello and Goodbye

Either Lemmen was crazy or the empty storefront used to be the Butterfly Bar. He put his hand through the metal grating and touched the window, but there was no outline of the golden words once etched there; inside it was only four walls, bits of plaster on the floor, a hole in the ceiling where there used to be a chandelier.

Yes, this was the same claustrophobic alley, no mistaking it; at the other end, that was Tu Do Street. The alley was half mud, half cracked pavement, with rickety wooden staircases leading to the back doors of second-story apartments. The sun never shone directly here, and it smelled like moldy garbage and stale urine. All the stores and stands were empty. The only thing moving was a chicken, pecking at the side of the pavement.

Lemmen walked slowly down the alley, touching things. A shoeshine stand was empty; it never had been much more than a doorway. Lemmen remembered the kid who had worked here, wondered what had happened to him, which led to thoughts of Van. The thought of getting that kid out of the swamp kept recurring to him. Maybe

Command could help. He'd get to work on that the minute he got back to Delta Town. Except that the strangest
thought came to him—what if he got back and Delta
Town wasn't there? What kind of crazy thought is that,
Lemmen? he said to himself, and walked farther into the
alley.

Used to be a souvenir stand out on the pavement and
when Lemmen got to it there was an old lady, way back in
the stall. She had filmy eyes. Lemmen thought it might be
the same lady from years ago, but she didn't recognize
him. She could barely see anything, looked only vaguely
in his direction. She sold no blue jeans, no army medals,
no cassette tapes, no rock 'n' roll posters. Her one table
held bolts of cloth—black, mostly, with a few remnants of
dark purple.

The lady said something Lemmen didn't understand; he
said, Hello, Grandmother, in Vietnamese. She was still
looking only vaguely at him, had a narrow face, full of sun
wrinkles and a deep tan. Certainly she didn't get that in
this alley—maybe she wasn't the woman from years ago.
Lemmen tried to form questions in his mind: about the
shoeshine boy; about Sharon and Sue and the Butterfly.
But the woman would not come forward more than a step.
She said something short and sharp to him, of which he
caught one word: *didi.*

"*Xin loi,*" he said—apologizing for what, he didn't
know, but he backed away, turned around, started walking, and when he was opposite the old Butterfly again, he
sat on wooden steps. They were mildewed, damp enough
that he could feel it through his uniform. The steps led to
the rooms once used by Sharon and Sue and all the Butterfly's girls. He looked back over his shoulder; the louver
windows were shut tight, no curtains, nobody home.

It was uncommonly quiet. He kept thinking about
Sharon and Sue. He didn't know their real names, first or
last; Saigon bar girls wouldn't tell you. He thought about
the fun he'd had with them, and that made him feel good;

but, of course, it wasn't fun for them, just money; and fooling around with them had cost him the best assignment he'd ever had, along with thirty nasty days of KP. But then, that had brought him to Delta Town, and the leadership of a grunt squad, which had taught him something he wouldn't have learned in twenty years in Little America. Now what exactly had he found out, and what was it worth to him?

He looked through that storefront glass as if he could see Sharon and Sue. Sue was the poorest girl he had ever known, judging from her bad teeth, and Sharon the bitchiest, because she went at it so hard; she was all eye makeup and purple fingernails, and in bed she bit and moaned—it was an act, and a very efficient one, Lemmen realized that now. Sharon was like a taxi driver, the quicker she got you there, the better for her. But Sue, she was genuinely sweet and shy, and always smelled of marijuana and seemed glassy-eyed—maybe it was the only way she could do her job, a thought that hadn't occurred to Lemmen before.

Now he realized that was all he knew about those girls, how they acted in their lives as whores. Why did he want to know more? He was just another customer, and the whole thing was only temporary for everybody—but somehow that made him feel bad. There should have been something more noble in it somewhere.

He was distracted by a flash of color, dark red, the chicken pecking in the mud near him. Lemmen lobbed a chunk of asphalt toward the bird; it squawked and flapped and moved on, still pecking. Lemmen stood, said a good-bye to Sharon and Sue, wherever they were, and wished them luck. Then walked toward the sunlight of Tu Do Street.

Only it didn't look like the old Tu Do Street; most of the stalls and shops and all the bars were closed. Of course, it was early, but in the old days this street was nonstop GI—twenty-four hours a day of drinking, shouting, screwing, and spending. This morning, mothers and children hud-

dled in doorways; young drunks and opium fiends lay like
the dead, in filthy gutters; silent old men squatted together
sharing one stub of a cigarette; ragamuffins crossed the
street, mumbling "GI" and "Souvenir me," and that's
when Lemmen realized he'd given his last dollar to
Nuong. Didn't even have a quarter on him. He had to
walk a zigzag path to avoid stepping on anyone. From the
storefront of a closed bar, a boy with a misshapen face—all
nose and forehead—said, "GI! You buy scag?"

He hurried toward the boulevard. No Saigon cowboys
drove by—there was no one worth stealing from anymore.
There were no trucks full of horny, wild young soldiers,
no jeeps carrying stern-faced MPs. It was hotter already,
and he was sweating, and as he got to the boulevard, he
heard traffic noise: the beeps of cyclos, the bells of rickshaws, the squeal of tires.

But even on the boulevard, things weren't the same.
The buildings were modern, green and glassy—could have
been Dallas or Miami—but everywhere were listless, rag-
ged people who looked as if they'd just come in from some
village; they camped under pieces of cardboard, crowded
on rugs and mats, huddled under canvas held up by sticks;
babies and children and old men, and women of every age,
they lay on the lawns of hotels and banks, they squatted
on sidewalks, and Lemmen had to walk in the street, dodg-
ing cyclos and rickshaws and the occasional battered
Toyota or Citroën.

Up one block was Worthington's building, an older,
moldy-concrete hotel that had become the U.S. Advisor
Corps Communication Center, with a big sign that said so.
Its lower courtyard and each balcony were draped with
grenade screens. Living in the shade of the mildewed
courtyard wall were women in black clothing and conical
hats, old men with hardly any flesh on them, crying children bothered by swarms of flies. A black MP was squatting, helping a woman calm a squalling baby as Lemmen
walked to the gateway, waved, and went through.

In the courtyard was a swimming pool, covered with mildewed plywood. A few café tables were pushed aside, umbrellas rotted. Trees and bushes were dying all around the courtyard walls. This must have been a nice place to have a drink once, Lemmen thought, but then gathered himself for business. He walked into an empty lobby, nobody at the desk, just a list, written in grease pencil on a white plastic slate. Worthington on six. No elevator service.

He climbed the narrow tiled stairway, passing barred windows on the landings. He reviewed his strategy. He'd come early to catch Worthington sober. He would use the early hour as an excuse to decline a drink—at least until the important things were taken care of. A slot for him in Saigon, that was the big thing. He could almost hear Worthington saying, "Son of a bitch," as he opened the door, almost hear himself making the pitch, almost hear Worthington saying, "We'll work something out, leave it to the old sarge," Worthington could work this army bureaucracy; and he loved to show how he could get things done.

Third floor and Lemmen stopped, huffing, told himself to slow down. He imagined old Worthington: the shrewdest face Lemmen had ever seen, with pale blue eyes that could stare down an officer, hide a straight flush, search out an obscure regulation. When Lemmen first met Worthington, he'd felt as if a light had gone on in some dark closet of his mind. This man was all army. He seemed to know everything: where to change money, how to sneak a jeep out the main gate, where to eat, where to get laid, which assignments were choice, which where hard and dangerous. He believed in no one and nothing but himself, and told that to anyone who would listen. On the evening of Lemmen's first day on the job, Worthington had taken him to the club for a few drinks, to ask how he liked it. Lemmen had given a careful answer, meant to please. He said he had come over here to fight the Communists, but if this was where the army needed him, he'd do his duty.

Fight the Communists! Worthington had shouted, and nearly spilled his drink. Where'd you get a goddamn cornball idea like that? Let me tell you something, son: You're not here to fight the Communists, you're here to have fun.

Which proved to be true, at least for Worthington, Lemmen thought, and started climbing stairs again. While some guys were sweating inside an APC, riding through the bush toward who knew what, Worthington sat, feet on his desk, in air-conditioned comfort; while some grunt in the Delta waded a leech-infested river, Worthington soaped himself in a hot shower. While some nervous squad —Lemmen's squad—had been dropped by a slick into a hot LZ, Worthington had been in a rickshaw headed toward Tu Do Street. Worthington was no fool! Lemmen wondered, for maybe the hundredth time, about the rumors of Worthington's fondness for Vietnamese boys. But Worthington seemed all man! Then why were the rumors so persistent? Had he ever seen Worthington with a girl? No. Had Worthington made a hint of a sexual advance toward Lemmen or anyone Lemmen had ever known? No. It was confusing; Lemmen climbed the stairs and dismissed it from his mind.

He reached the sixth floor and stopped at the window a moment, looking over this part of Saigon, and what he noticed wasn't the buildings but the roads: they were crowded with people, carts, and water buffalo, making long, narrow clouds of dust all the way to the horizon.

Worthington would know what was happening. Probably he'd say: Don't mean a damn thing, Lemmen. Just another panic. Happens every few months. Lemmen knew it was a well-worked VC trick, to frighten the peasants out of the villages and send them into Saigon, where they'd be miserable and cause trouble.

Lemmen turned the corner and walked down the corridor, looking for 614, and when he got there, the door was shut, and the whole corridor was silent, and suddenly Lemmen noticed what had been there all along: a yellow tape across the door that said: CID. DO NOT CROSS. On the door itself was a handwritten note:

Services for FSGT Worthington
will be held at 0800 hours Friday
in the main chapel at Little America.

"Services!" Lemmen said. He couldn't take his eyes off that word. He knocked on the door, nothing; went to the next door and knocked on it, no answer; then he ran down the stairs saying "Services!" and when he got to the lobby he realized why the corridor had been empty, it was just after eight and it was Friday, he took Nuong's watch out of his pocket to confirm that, and ran out the courtyard and past the gate to where the MP was talking to the Vietnamese along the wall.

"I'm a friend of First Sergeant Worthington's," Lemmen said; couldn't get his breath. "What happened?"

The MP stood up. "Sorry to tell you this, Sergeant, but old man Worthington, he went and blew his brains out."

Lemmen felt himself falling and sat down among the refugees.

Hoa made tea. Or so the major insisted on calling it. Well, if he called it tea, she would call it tea, but it smelled of iodine and had the color of river water. The major had strange habits. He drank strong coffee day and night, right until bedtime. Special fancy coffee his wife sent from the United States, a pound a week. The major absolutely despised tea. Still, he owned a large, gleaming silver tea tray with a matching teapot, elegant containers for cream and sugar, eight delicate cups and saucers, and a dozen heavy spoons. He kept the set behind glass doors in a tall wooden cabinet, along with bottles of liquor he never drank, old hunting rifles he never fired, framed photos of a pretty daughter he never bragged about, and plaques and trophies he never admired. Sometimes, when there wasn't much to do in the trailer, the major would ask Hoa to do certain nothing jobs, and one of them was to polish the tea set. Hoa would always do it, of course, but not without cursing under her breath, not without wondering why the major fussed so much over things he never used.

But this morning it did begin to make sense, Hoa admitted that. She should have realized that the tea set was kept for important people. Such as this old, almost crippled man who wore hearing aids on both ears. Who was sitting in the major's front room. Along with a tall, slender woman who could not be more than thirty years old but already had fully gray hair. Of course, she was pretty— every American girl Hoa had ever seen was pretty. Hoa looked over her shoulder and into the front room. She locked in the woman's slate-gray eyes, then looked away. Her fingers touched the waistband of her black trousers. Felt a reassuring crinkle, the envelope of her letter to Bill. She put three teabags into the silver pot, wrapped a towel around her hand, and took a saucepan of boiling water from the stove. Arms shaking with the weight of the pan, she slowly poured the water into the teapot, then stepped back from the smelly steam.

Hoa glanced at the coffeepot to make sure it was percolating. The major wanted coffee handy, in case he needed it. Because of his problem—his habit of falling asleep while he was listening to people. He could stay awake just fine when he was talking, but when someone spoke to him, the major's eyes might start to close; if he was standing he'd quickly need a place to lie or sit. The major had a name for these sleep fits; he called them his little naps. Well, this morning he had asked Hoa to brew pot after pot of coffee, and drank it almost as fast as she could boil water. Twice he'd said to her: Can't be taking one of my little naps when the congressman's here, can I?

Well, now the important people were here and the major was staying awake just fine. He had driven his guests all around Delta Town and when they came back, to Hoa's surprise they had Bill with them. She didn't know he'd come back from Saigon! Bill was last in the door, his hat in his hand; Bill, who was almost as big as all three of them put together. Bill, who looked so rough—compared to the major in his crisp, starchy uniform, to the old man in white shirt and polished black shoes, to the gray-haired woman, who wore a dress and white stockings.

Hoa would wait a bit for the tea to brew. She had filled silver bowls with sugar cubes, lemons, and cream, had spread a paper doily on the silver tray and arranged flat cookies in a nice semicircle. She took a towel and wiped four small cups and saucers spotless. And, of course, she listened.

"In your opinion, Sergeant Lemmen," the woman said, and then paused. "Colonel, you might answer this too . . ."

"Beg pardon," the major said. Hoa had never heard him so polite. "But it's major, ma'am."

"Of course," the woman said. "I'm afraid I'm confused. It's the *silver* oak leaf for colonel, isn't it? Well, Major, you might want to answer too. What evidence have you seen that the Vietnamese troops have the will to resist the Communists?"

Hoa did not fully understand the question. The major seemed to. "Well," he said, "as you observed a couple of days ago, men like Sergeant Lemmen here are going out to the boonies to bring the Arvin boys up to American fighting standards. It's all part of Operation Scarecrow. But hell, helping these people out, that's been our goal all along. Hasn't it, Sergeant?"

Hoa picked up the tray—how heavy!—and walked carefully, balanced on the balls of her feet, into the room.

"You say so, sir," Bill said.

"And in your opinion, Sergeant," the woman said, "are we succeeding in that goal?"

With a slight rattle, Hoa put the tea down on the low, round table in the middle of the four Americans.

"Well," the major said, "here's my little sweetheart with the tea. Thank you, darling. *Cam on ong.*" To the gray-haired woman he said, in lowered voice, "It pays to talk to them in their language." He looked at Hoa and winked. A signal that he was doing just fine. Hoa was to watch him for signs of sleepiness. If she saw his eyes definitely close, she was to touch his shoulder and say: Coffee, Major?

"Sir," the major said, very loudly, "tea?"

"Yes, yes," the old man with the hearing aids said. He was in the big reclining chair—the major called it his thinking chair. It was backed against a shelf of books. The major himself hardly ever sat in that chair, and Hoa had never seen him take down a book. But the old man had taken an interest in one of the books—a paperback. When he put it on his lap and bent forward for tea, Hoa saw the cover. It had a picture of a blond American woman, naked except for a red scarf, her privates covered by words of the title, which Hoa could not understand except for a big red-lipstick *O*.

They were all quiet now, only the rattling of cups and stirring of spoons. The old man in the chair of honor, the woman and the major widely separated on the couch, Bill on a kitchen chair. The woman uncrossed her legs so she could reach for a cookie. Hoa wondered whether this woman perhaps had an eye for Bill. Or Bill for her! How could she compete with a woman who dressed like that on a workday? The major took a cookie and popped it into his mouth. The woman bit into her cookie, made a sour face, and put it down.

"Sweetheart," the major said, "do you think you could come up with fresh cookies of some kind?"

Hoa just nodded. These people! Of course cookies were soggy in this weather. She turned for the kitchen, but the woman grabbed her by the wrist. "That's quite all right," the woman said to her. "Major, I do hope the working women on this base are accorded their full rights and dignity."

"Why, shoot," the major said. "Of course."

"I admit I had to wonder when I heard you call this woman 'sweetheart,' Major. It's so condescending."

"That's just a manner of speaking," the major said. "Why, this little girl here, I'm going to lose her in a couple of days. And do you know why? She's quitting me, she's going up to Saigon, where there's better opportunity. How's that for equal treatment?"

The woman let go of Hoa's wrist. "I'm in full solidarity with you," the woman said. Hoa backed away, rubbed her wrist—it was all red. She tried to figure it out—did they want fresh cookies or not?

She would have liked to look at Bill, to get a sign or flicker of the eyes from him. Maybe she should speak to him directly, what did she care, now that she was leaving the major? But this woman had a lock on Bill. She had a notebook in the lap of her dress, and looked down at it.

"We have an unanswered question here," the woman said. "I believe I asked you, Sergeant, since you are the one with firsthand experience at it, whether Operation Scarecrow was succeeding." Her eyes, her deep gray eyes, focused intensely on Bill's face. She was going to write down what he said!

"My personal opinion?" Bill said. He looked nervous. Why?

"Yes," the woman said.

"Well, personally," Bill said, and shifted in the chair. Reached for the teacup and sipped from it. It was shaking in his hands! He looked at the major, looked at the woman; they stared directly at him. He looked at the old man, who paid attention only to his book.

"I wish . . ." Bill said. Hoa noticed his Adam's apple, bobbing. He couldn't speak! He made noises in his throat. He coughed and recovered. "I wish you could have stayed out there with us, ma'am. Instead of flying over us in a helicopter. Then you would have seen for yourself."

"Would have seen what, Sergeant?" the woman asked, and then scribbled into her notebook.

"Disloyalty, ma'am."

"I beg your pardon?" the woman said.

"A soldier either follows orders, or he's a traitor."

"Why don't you tell me exactly what you're talking about, Sergeant."

"He's fatigued," the major said, and popped off the couch and glanced at the old man. Bill's hands were shaking—he jammed them into his pockets.

"I'd like to hear, Major," the woman said, "what this man has to say."

"Ma'am," Bill said, "could the congressman help me bring a Vietnamese orphan out of that swamp?"

"We were talking about United States policy," the woman said.

But Bill went on as if she had said nothing. "If he stays out there, one way or the other he'll die. I would like to request, sir, and sir . . ." He looked from the congressman to the major. "That he be brought in and sent to an orphanage where he'll be safe. He's only ten years old."

The congressman looked up from his book and smiled. The woman was scribbling furiously. Bill stood up and the major put his hand on his shoulders and said, kindly, "Thank you, Sergeant."

Bill glanced at Hoa, then stood straight and saluted the major, opened his mouth to say something, changed his mind, put his hat on, nodded to the woman, nodded to the congressman, and backed out the screen door.

But he stood outside holding the door open. "I'll do it myself, then," he said. "I'm going to do one decent thing before I leave here." He let the door bang shut. "One decent thing!" he shouted, and threw his boonie hat in the dust and walked away.

It was silent in the trailer until the woman said: "Well." That was all she said. The old man seemed small, almost lost in the big recliner. He looked left and right, rested the teacup on the book in his lap, smiled nicely. For an old man, Hoa noticed, he had wonderful white teeth. "What happened to that big young fellow?" the old man asked.

"Pressing duties," the major said, very loudly. The old man nodded, sipped.

"He never answered my question," the woman said.

"Well," the major said, speaking very low, "I'll have to get Sergeant Lemmen a few days off. He's had a history of alcohol problems, you know." The major shook his head. Looked at the old man, looked at the woman, raised his voice. "Now, we were talking about Operation Scarecrow, weren't we? More cookies?" he asked, then turned to Hoa: "Where are those cookies, darling?"

Things had changed, Lemmen could see that: something smoky and hazy and dusty about Vinh Long now. Of course, that could be in his brain, because the world got that way, hazy, when he'd downed enough bourbon. And he'd had plenty. He was riding in a cyclo-rickshaw, opening a fresh bottle, thinking about what it would be like to be a private E-2, mosquito wings on his shoulder. And this bust he'd deserve, for committing the biggest sin in the military: making your commander look bad. The bust he could take—but the transfer, never!

For three hours after leaving the major's trailer, he had sat on his bunk, drinking by himself, and somewhere in there he'd nodded off. When he woke up, sweating, there were two envelopes on his footlocker, a small white one on top of a long manila one. The white envelope held a letter from Hoa; in the manila one was green paper, official orders, handwritten by Command. He was to report for duty at Fort Carson, Colorado, in fifteen days.

He'd taken Hoa's letter, run to the main gate, and

caught a rickshaw for town. People along the market street seemed to be hustling. There were more cyclos, more three-wheeled buses, more rickshaws—everyone seemed to be headed north. Only a few old women were selling fish and vegetables from their tubs. Hardly any Arvin soldiers were in town. The old man parked the rickshaw at the traffic circle and Lemmen got out, pocketed his bottle, paid the fare; the old man, looking beat and sweaty, bowed to him and walked off to sit in the shade of a tree.

Already Lemmen could see something different about the Hello and Goodbye too. Sandbags! Piled around the walls, piled to the windows. The shutters were jammed shut. Lemmen stood in the doorway; there was a small sign in Vietnamese. He couldn't read it. Where was Hoa? To his right there was a clunk, and a shutter opened halfway. A face appeared in the shadows. A tiny pinched face, topped by a white helmet inscribed with the letters *QC.*

"Chao ong QC," Lemmen said, and looked past the soldier into the barroom. It was wrecked: the big mirror had been shattered, the bar overturned to block the doorway, the tables, chairs, and booths pushed to the walls.

"Where is everyone?" Lemmen asked.

"Didi," the QC said.

"I'm looking for my friend," Lemmen said.

"Didi mau," the QC said, his voice rising, almost breaking. Lemmen saw the tightness of the face, the flicker of hate. Heard a whipping sound, a .45 coming out of its holster. He backed up. "Have you seen Miss Muon?" he asked.

The QC pointed the pistol, and Lemmen felt a shock go through his body, and twisted away, ran close along the storefronts, ducked into one, looked back at the Hello and Goodbye. Maybe she was in her room. He cupped his hands around his mouth. "Hoa!" he yelled.

A gunshot. The bullet ricocheted in the street and Lemmen crouched, waited for a second shot, and when it didn't come he ran around the corner.

He stood in an alleyway that led to the Mekong, breathing heavy and trying to think. If the QCs had Hoa back there, she would have answered. From his top pocket he took out the sheet of almost transparent paper that Hoa had covered with tiny, graceful writing. He looked it over, as if now, somehow, he would magically discover its meaning. A feverish scan and he saw no word he could translate. Even her name—what did it mean? Those little marks—he'd tried to learn them but could never get them straight—they changed the meaning entirely. Even a simple word, like Hoa's name, could mean flower, or could mean to transform something, or to equal the score, or to mix and mingle. It could mean peace, fire, misfortune— God damn it. He stuffed the letter back into his pocket, checked Nuong's watch; Hoa had been off work for hours.

Disaster! He could feel it coming, and suddenly he took off running for the traffic circle, and hopped onto the rickshaw's cyclo, turned the key, zoomed away. He glanced back once to see the old man, waving his arms, almost lost in a cloud of dust and exhaust. Lemmen whipped past the fishwomen, the rice warehouse, the soccer field, the ruined schoolhouse; he made a sharp, loud, dust-spitting turn down a dirt path, leaned forward on the scooter, put his head down; his right hand nearly breaking the throttle off, he roared down the path, praying for no tripwires, dust in his face, bouncing over holes in the road, riding furiously through tunnels of vegetation then out to flat, wide rice paddy vistas then into green tunnels again and finally into the village clearing; he hit the brake with his heel and the bike spun, broke free of the carriage, tumbled to a stop, wheels spinning, dust everywhere. He lay for a second, staring at a chicken coop. White feathers caught in the wires.

Then he passed out.

He woke up in the dark in his underwear. The only light was dull red, a glass-covered candle in front of a tiny altar. Slowly, Lemmen realized where he was: lying on a dirt floor in a Vietnamese hut. Hoa humming, squatting next to him. To Lemmen for a moment she was a vision: her straw conical hat at the back of her head, held in place by a purple ribbon that crossed low on her skinny throat just at the veins; her bony face and slightly flat nose; her naturally red lips, pursed as she hummed; the black curls at her forehead, the long eyelashes, which did a slow blink —then she looked straight at him.

"You!" she said. She reached out and touched his face. Caressed it, cool hands. "Why?" she asked.

Lemmen started to sit up. He grimaced: pain.

"No," she said, and put her hand on his chest, as if she were strong enough to push him down. When Lemmen sat up anyway, she moved her hand to strawberry-red scrape marks on the outside of his thigh.

"Troi oi," she said.

Lemmen started to touch it but she slapped his hand away. She put her fingers to her mouth; she brought them down wet with saliva and drew her fingertips over the wounds. Lemmen winced, expecting pain; felt none. He realized she'd been doing this for a while.

"Did you see my letter?" she asked.

"Hoa, I can't read it."

"Sergeant Nuong," she said.

"Nuong is—" Lemmen said, then realized he didn't want to say "gone." "He's with his family. I don't know if he'll be back. Ouch!" He pushed her hand away from the sore. Leaned in toward her. Put his hand at the back of her hat, brought her face near his, kissed her on the lips. "I was worried," he said. "The Hello and Goodbye is sandbagged, there's a QC there, what's going on?"

"Goddamn QCs," Hoa said. And drew back, her face with a sudden mean look to it.

"I had a bottle in my pants pocket," Lemmen said.

Hoa leaned backward and drew it out of his folded, ripped trousers.

"I need a drink," he said.

"You do not," she said. "But I will give it to you anyway." She handed him a nearly full pint of Grand-dad. "Lucky for you it did not break and cut you."

"Lucky," Lemmen said, and took a sip. "Here's to the goddamn QCs. One of them shot at me."

Hoa did not seem surprised. "They are bastards," she said.

"Why did you write the letter?" Lemmen asked. "Why are you quitting the major? What's this about going to Saigon?"

"Things are now happening," Hoa said. She would not look in his eyes.

"What do you mean by 'things'?"

He saw that look he'd seen enough times in this country, the eyes of an iron-willed fanatic. "You have waited too long!" she shouted. More quietly, she said: "I am going to my mother in Saigon."

Lemmen breathed out hard, realizing that somehow he had failed her. "Maybe that will be good," he said.

"No," she said.

"What do you mean, no?"

"You do not understand. I am going back to my family." She pushed away from him and stood. Lemmen had a flash, seeing her, full length, in black pajamas, purple blouse, conical hat—a Vietnamese peasant. A revelation! She speaks English and listens to rock 'n' roll but she's a rice paddy girl. Why hadn't he ever seen that in the Hello and Goodbye? He took a long look at her and said: "The major has transferred me to the States."

"He told me. He made me bring the papers to you. You were sleeping." She waved her hand in front of her nose. "You smelled drunk."

"Maybe we should try to get married," Lemmen said.

"Now you say!" she shouted. "It is too late. My brother is on his way. Too late! Damn you!" She picked up her bedroll and with both hands smashed it hard into his chest. It bounced off, rolled to her feet. She kicked it. "Damn you!" she yelled.

Lemmen grabbed the bedroll, spread it out. Found he was lying on a towel—a big white towel from the Hello and Goodbye. He stood and wrapped it around his waist. Hoa was squatting in the doorway, looking out into darkness. Maybe she wanted to run away, but where could she go? At night you were trapped inside. He went behind her, took off her hat gently. Put it point-side down on the floor. His hands went around her waist to her stomach. He held her close. She did not respond or resist.

He kissed the back of her hair. She turned toward him, offered her face and lips. He kissed her and led her back to the bedroll. Brought her down with him.

"I am telling you, I must go to Saigon," she said. "I would have gone this morning if my brother had come on time."

"Just let me keep my arms around you for a while," he said.

"My brother will be here any time."

"I don't want you to go with him," Lemmen said.

"I am going anyway."

"Just lie here with me."

They lay together, and after a while Hoa stopped squirming and they were still and peaceful, listening to sounds of the Delta night outside: a symphony of frogs, insects, and lizards. After a while Hoa started humming, her voice beautiful in his ears.

"What are you humming?" Lemmen asked.

"I am happy for now," she said.

"That's the name of the song?" Lemmen asked.

"No," she said. "You would not know the name. It is a small village song."

"Why don't you sing the words?"

"You would not understand this song," she said.

"Go ahead, sing it anyway."

Lemmen woke up sober under an army blanket with a dry, hollow feeling. He could see almost nothing, the darkness helped only by moonlight leaking in the openings that were doors and windows; the altar candle had gone out. He reached for Hoa. She was asleep in all her clothes, lying curled and warm with her back to him. He rubbed his hand gently along her skinny arm, skinny ribs, skinny hips and legs. Kissed the hair on the back of her head lightly. Her hair had a wiry texture and smelled wonderful; homemade soap.

He sat up, packed the blanket carefully around her. Felt around on the dirt floor until he touched fabric, his pants, pulled them to him. The pint of Grand-dad in there, almost half left in it. He held it up to the window; he decided he'd had enough for a while.

He stood and took a deep, slow breath. So this, he thought, is it. The tropical countryside. He loved the smell of the air. GIs who didn't know better said this country stank, but that was fertility, by God. Out of that slimy smell and paddy muck came this beautiful, lush, productive land. Where people kept the practices of their ancestors for time out of mind. Where concrete and plastic hardly existed. Where people lived in houses built from the straw of their own harvest, used buffalo to plow their land, ate what they grew in their own fields, plus chickens or pigs if they slaughtered them, fish if they could catch them. Water? They collected rain in big jars. Wine? They fermented rice. The honesty of it. The simplicity of it. How lucky, these people who could call it home.

Lemmen walked, barefoot, toward the window. He stepped on a flat piece of wood, a hollow sound came from underneath it. It was the entrance to the family bomb shelter, dug under the floor, and down a few feet to just above the water table. Stepping on that board made Lemmen realize something, some flaw in his thinking. Ugliness, hatred, insane cruelty, all of it was out there too: the Viet Cong, the booby traps, the rice paddies full of graves.

That VC scout out in the swamp—had Lemmen killed the guy by accident with a mortar round, or had he snuck up on the camp at night, and caught the blast of Nuong's claymore? It was hard to know for sure. Either way, that guy had only been a loyal soldier, following orders and doing his duty.

Which was what? To set up the people in Post Twelve for slaughter. So why should Lemmen feel sorry for him? Another dead guy. So what? This was a war.

Or was it a game?

Lemmen had a vision of Post Twelve as it might be, this morning or any day soon: smoking and in ruins, the bloody bodies of men, women, and children—Van!—lying in the mud. He remembered the rasping sound of Holloway's wound, Buck's bloody shirt, Carney's face bloated beyond human features. It was a war all right.

He remembered Worthington, pulling strings in Little America; the days he himself had played God standing in the tower, reading names, sending newbies to who knew what fate; he remembered Command, flying over the swamp with a half-deaf congressman in the backseat. It was a game all right.

He lit a cigarette and leaned on the windowsill—not too hard, these houses were fragile. What was the use of thinking about it? All his thoughts went in circles. There was no undoing what had been done. He looked out into the moonlit night, listened to the light rhythm of Hoa, breathing. Listened to the lizards chirping, frogs croaking, insects whirring.

What could he possibly do? A career man had to follow orders, unless they were illegal, but everything Lemmen had ever been ordered to do was perfectly legal. Fire mortar rounds at someone's village—legal. Take a bunch of teenage draftees on a suicide mission to assault dug-in NVA machine gunners—legal. Enter a village, line people up at gunpoint while you searched their houses—legal. Sit alongside a trail all night waiting for someone to walk down it so you could murder them—nothing more legal in the world.

So where did all this thinking lead him? Nowhere. He was headed for Fort Carson, that was all he knew, unless some miracle happened.

What would happen to Hoa when he was gone? He watched the dirt trail in the moonlight. What a shame— the whole village all abandoned huts. Except for that old guy, Mister Ma, across the way, still keeping chickens. For the purpose, Hoa said, of bribing whichever side won control of the village. Once she had imitated him, squinching her face and talking in her deepest voice: Here, I am an old man, in need of food, but I will give you this chicken because your cause is just. Over the years, Hoa had said, the old man had given chickens to the French Foreign Legion, the Viet Minh, the Arvin Rangers, the Green Berets, the American 9th Division, the Cao Dai militia, the Arvin 9th Division, the Hoa Haos, the British, the Viet Cong, the Koreans, the People's Self-Defense Force, the Australians, the QCs, the Japanese, the American 1st Aviation Brigade—once he gave a half-dead rooster to a stray patrol of Algerians.

Lemmen saw a glint in the window of that house—Mister Ma watching him. Hoa had said that Mister Ma had come out when Lemmen had crashed, had helped Hoa walk him into the house—then had started a barrage of questions, which Hoa had answered with evasions. Lemmen couldn't remember any of it. He saw Mister Ma strike some tiny light inside his house. The old bastard, Lemmen thought, he might even report them to the QCs —him for the crime of stealing a rickshaw, her for the crime of sleeping with an American.

Maybe he should file papers now to marry Hoa, and get her sent to the States. That would give him time to work through his Fort Carson tour—in a year or two they'd be back, maybe he could settle for Saigon. But how to get around the six-month wait for a marriage license? Command could get it done, but there was no way the major would do him a favor now. Worthington could have done it. Lemmen smoked and stared out into the darkness, and thought about how little he must have known about Worthington. All the ghosts in this country!

He couldn't stay inside any longer—he'd have to walk around and think things over. It's not so dangerous, he told himself, there haven't been any VC here in years.

He knelt at Hoa's side. She came awake some, rolled on her back, and Lemmen kissed her on the lips. "What are you doing?" she asked.

"Sleep," he said. "I'm all right. Sleep." He passed his hand lightly over her face to close her eyes. She sighed and curled on her side.

He got his trousers on, lit another Lucky. Went out to what served as a porch—bamboo poles with a straw roof. He cuffed the cigarette. Nuong! How had Nuong gotten his family out? Who was taking money for the boat captains off Vung Tau? If only he had thought to ask Nuong.

He walked to the end of the porch, ducked under the

bamboo rail, and stood on the trail. Stubbed his cigarette out on the ground. Then field-stripped it, out of habit, reducing it to tobacco flecks and the tiniest ball of paper.

He walked barefoot past Mister Ma's home to the edge of the clearing where it was dark trees and bushes. He could smell the mountain apples. Mister Ma was watching from a window, Lemmen knew it. To hell with the dream of living in the Delta, he thought. People like Mister Ma, with their snooping ways, ruined life in a small village— no wonder Hoa had moved to town.

He made noise going into the bush, found the tree by feel, groped until he found one little apple, then another. He stepped out on the trail and ate a whole apple in one bite, seeds and everything.

What a country! A man walks out his door, picks a snack off a tree. Lemmen chewed the other apple. Wonderful burst of juice in his mouth. Was there anything in the world that didn't grow or live here? A storybook land. Tigers, elephants, monkeys, snakes—everything. He walked along the trail. A banana grove was down there a way. He had no weapon, but he didn't want one. Just once he wanted to walk somewhere in this country without a rifle in his hand.

He walked down the trail, hands in his pockets, to the banana grove—it was bright in the moonlight. He went to the shortest tree, no higher than he was, and reached in for a banana. Peeled it. Ate it; warm and fragrant and delicious. He walked toward the river. Amazing what you could smell in this country at night: the river, the rice, the fruit, the muck.

Under trees it became totally black; night really meant something here. When it was night, it was dark and dangerous for eleven hours, and everyone but soldiers and criminals stayed home. No lights anywhere: no gas stations, no supermarkets, no neon signs, no headlights, no streetlights, no lights in the windows of homes, except for those of busybodies like Mister Ma; it was all as it was meant to be—when you looked up, the stars shone like little moons.

At an open field he passed a dark rectangle before he realized what it was: a concrete mausoleum. They buried a man on the best part of his land. That idea comforted Lemmen. Great-grandfather, grandfather, father, and son, all in one place. People lived among familiar things all their lives—the river, the paddies, the animals—and most of them never traveled any farther than the market street. They didn't want to. Didn't need to! Everything right here. Timeless and changeless, buffalo, plows, hard work, sun, rain, family, God.

Lemmen walked, losing himself in thoughts like that, then got a chill, remembering that Charley liked to hide behind those mausoleums. He walked more softly, bare feet silent on the trail. Then he was right up on it, the Mekong. Silvery black and ripply, reflecting moonlight in its tiny waves. Afloat with logs and branches and gigantic bunches of lily pads, some as big as a barge. Lemmen sat on the bank. Tide high; his feet dangled at the surface of the water. What a river! As wide and strong as the Mississippi—but warm! Never frozen. No goo in it—except for nature's goo. Lemmen wished with every part of his heart that he'd been a boy here. He'd watched these boys many times, with envy: how they trapped frogs, caught fish, swam and splashed in the river, pissed in it, played in it, brushed their teeth in it—which made Lemmen remember the Mississippi: nobody swam in it, nobody would dare eat fish from it, a river of barges and factories. He let his feet dangle in the Mekong. He felt perfectly fine for a few minutes; he watched a giant lily pad cluster float toward the sea.

Which gave him a new and daring idea. Behind him somewhere, a rooster crowed.

Late-Blooming Flower

The sidewalk was overflowing with people when Hoa bumped into Ba the bar-mother. The people, women mostly, were not milling about as on an ordinary market day; they went in one direction, like a river, carrying net bags, cardboard boxes, kerchief bundles; they led small children. They bought furiously from besieged fishwomen who squatted alongside their galvanized tubs under big umbrellas. Hoa did not bump into Ba, actually, but into her fish tub.

Ba was selling shrimp! At first Hoa could not believe her eyes—Ba who once made hundreds of piasters a day running a girl bar, who had bought that business from the profits of giving tarot card readings in her home along the highway. Now she was a fishwoman! At first Ba did not notice Hoa. She squatted, listening to a radio, her hair wrapped in a kerchief.

Hoa said, Auntie!

Ba turned and pursed her lips—a sign to be quiet while she listened to the radio. She acted as if it were no surprise that she had reappeared in town in a new and humble occupation. Hoa squatted in the shade of the umbrella. She took off her hat, put it at her feet, dropped her kerchief bundle. In Ba's tub were a few sick, blue-looking shrimp sunk in gray water.

Why are you still down here? Ba asked. She hardly glanced away from the radio.

Hoa did not answer; she was staring. She had to get used to the idea that Ba was back. She found herself admiring the silvery-gray hair that stuck out from Ba's kerchief; she had always hoped to look that nice when she was old. Ba had gorgeous skin too: brown but not too dark, and very smooth. She had not spent her life in the paddies—or she would be dark and wrinkled and used up. Unlike Hoa's mother, Ba had not become a crushed widow when she lost her husband—she went out and became rich! Now Ba was dressed plainly, in black trousers and a white blouse, but still she looked like royalty—except for her hands, which were full of cuts and scabs from the fish knife.

Where is your GI friend? Ba asked. Has he left you?

My GI friend is over there waiting for me, Hoa said. She stood and looked over the heads of haggling women to see Bill, who was in the shadow of an army truck that had stalled on the road. Bill was talking to a Vietnamese soldier who had the truck's hood raised, and had his head in the engine compartment.

Auntie, Hoa said, and squatted again. How is it you have come back and where were you?

Ba looked at her for a moment and said: I had a dream.

What kind of dream?

A dream I was being watched over by soldiers.

Hoa watched her eyes for a moment; there seemed to be something she didn't want to say. Why did she avoid the look of Hoa's eyes?

Auntie, Hoa said, I'm so glad I saw you. I would like you to tell my fortune.

Ba looked down as if she were staring into her trousers.

On the radio, a woman talked in high, excited words. Hoa spoke again, louder. I have an important thing to decide, she said. My boyfriend wants me to stay with him, but I am thinking of going to find my mother.

Stay here? Ba said. He is crazy.

He told me this morning of his plan to get away.

Where is he going to run to?

To the sea, Auntie.

Late-Blooming Flower, Ba said, and sighed. I do not have my cards, so I cannot give you a proper reading. She put her scarred hand over Hoa's hand; it made Hoa's look pale, almost like porcelain.

Late Bloomer, she said, you do not need a reading when you can see: The streets are filled with people—and listen to the radio!

I have heard nothing on the radio, Hoa said.

Well, they have been saying all morning that the Northerners are fighting and the National Army is running. The Americans have said they will not come back. It is all here on the radio, every bit of it.

Hoa listened. The voice that came out of the little radio was shrill, and hard on the ears with its northern accent. It was the woman the GIs called Ho Chi Minnie, only now she was speaking from the Vietnamese side of her mouth.

It is no use anymore to struggle, the voice said, there has already been so much suffering for our poor nation. Isn't it time, fellow patriots, that we embraced each other in peace and fellowship? Now that all the foreigners have finally gone home, what have we to fight about? The Peace Council is offering the most generous terms for our reconciliation. Let us not waste another drop of Vietnamese blood or another Vietnamese tear. . . .

It is just Radio Hanoi, Hoa said. They have been broadcasting such lies since I was small.

Oh, yes, they lie all the time, said Ba. See how they promise to treat Southerners with courtesy? That is a lie not even a baby would believe. But are they lying about the National Army running away? Perhaps not. They mix lies and truth so well, it is hard to tell.

Dial in the GI radio, Hoa said.

Ba's lips turned down; she ran her hand over the dial and paused at the music of American guitars; then she turned back to the Vietnamese station. How can we tell down here, in this little town, what is going on? she said. But look at the highway and see these miserable people walking all the way from Can Tho and Soc Trang—they must know something to make them abandon their villages and flee a hundred miles.

She put her hand to Hoa's face, stroked it. Flower, she said, I have no prediction for you, only guesses from what I hear on lying radios—and I cannot get my tarot cards. I have destroyed them. When the inquisitors come to my home, they will find nothing but my fish tub and kerchief.

She played with Hoa's hair, curled it around her finger. Tell me, she said, does the American have honest intent to you?

I believe he cares for me, Hoa said.

Either way, Flower, you are taking a chance. I hear they are starving in Saigon, all the road people. Country people don't stand a chance up there—has your mother gotten herself a place there yet?

I got a letter, Hoa said, but she had no address. Perhaps she has one now.

Perhaps she is still on the streets. And where is your brother?

He was supposed to come from Can Tho, Hoa said. I do not know what has kept him.

It is all very chancy, Ba said. You might be safer with the American—if he can get you out.

She heard her name shouted—Bill's loud voice. Bill's face, out in the sun, above the heads of the fishwomen. "Come on, Hoa—we have a ride!"

He was waving frantically. Somehow he must have

helped the Arvin soldier start his truck; the engine made blue smoke, and a horrid noise. Hoa said, I will go now, Auntie, and I will think. She came out of her squat, picked up her bundle. I love you, Auntie, she said.

Ba would not look her in the eyes. You were in the dream, Flower, she said. You and I were tending the side of the road, under the eyes of soldiers. The soldiers were smoking cigarettes and had their rifles slung very low. We were older and both of us had gray hair.

Suddenly, Bill reached in and grabbed Hoa by the shoulder, he did not seem to recognize Ba, or say anything to her, but pulled Hoa through the crowd to the truck, with its revving engine. He picked her up, put her in the back among dozens of people under a canvas roof. There were pigs and chickens and belongings in there too. Bill swung himself up, sat and held her at the edge of the tailgate, and she had to hold tight to a canvas strap as the truck drove through the crowd, beeping.

On both sides of the road they passed people who seemed to be sleepwalking. None of them turned or even looked up as the truck drove by. It was strange to see them from this backward view, all being left behind. The town itself faded as they passed a strip of countryside—fields, and in them a few sick, skinny cattle. Nobody in the truck spoke. Pigs snorted, chickens cackled. Babies cried and whined.

In a few minutes the truck jerked to a stop in front of the GI gate, which someone had reinforced with giant X's built of railroad ties, and with sandbags piled chest-high. Bill hopped out.

"Get down," he said, and held both hands up for her.

"You said we were going to go away."

"Not now," Bill said, his hands still up. "Will you get down?"

"Is this truck going for Saigon?"

"Yes, but we can't go yet, Hoa. Now get down."

She held on to the canvas strap and shook her head.

For a moment they looked at each other and the truck driver revved his engine. Bill reached for her and she backed away. Bill grabbed the tailgate as if he were going to swing himself up, but the truck started moving and he had to run just to hold on. The truck gained speed and the people in back of Hoa were murmuring and Bill was holding on and running, huffing, not saying anything, and in a moment he had to let go, and he was waving his arms, standing in the middle of the road, and Hoa glanced in back of her, all those people, crowded and dressed in such rags; she became afraid that this truck wasn't going to Saigon after all, maybe it was going someplace strange— maybe a relocation camp! She remembered Ba's dream, and when she looked out again, Bill was far down the road and fading. She got up, holding the strap in one hand and her kerchief bundle in the other, and shouted for the driver to stop.

All day Hoa had been nervous and sweaty, and now in the twilight she had a bad feeling in her stomach—as if worms were crawling around. Twice she had started to run away; the last time she got within sight of the main gate before she turned around. That was about five o'clock, with the sun already sinking, and what she saw was a crowd of road people pressed against the gate, clamoring to get in; Bill, with a squad of Arvins, stood behind the gate, keeping people out. If they are begging to get in, they must think it's safer here, Hoa told herself.

She turned on the light. She had never lived in a place with lights until the Hello and Goodbye—but the good thing about American lights was that they worked every time. Even the better people of Vinh Long, who had enjoyed lights for years, never knew what would happen when they threw the switch. America, Hoa thought, must be a land where everything worked every time.

Already she had turned Bill's big radio on and off about twenty times; now she sat on Bill's bunk—which was a mess when she had come in but was nicely made now—

and dialed it again. She passed every local station; the Hanoi and Saigon stations played fewer and fewer songs and had more and more announcers telling lies. She raised the antennas and kept dialing. The radio was a shortwave, and could get the whole world, or so it was claimed—it had a map of the world on its handle—but no matter how Hoa twisted the antennas, only static came in.

She shut off the radio, went to Bill's wall locker, and looked in: four bottles of bourbon on the top shelf and two white cartons of cigarettes; shirts and trousers hanging from a rod, and on the bottom shelf, extra boots, hand grenades, ammunition clips. Taped inside the door was a picture of Bill and Sergeant Nuong in the barracks, with Bill leaning forward into the camera and making a funny, mean face; Bill was three times the size of Nuong; he looked happy and drunk, and Nuong looked serious, with his one skewed eye. Underneath that was a foldout picture of an American girl, naked and proud of her large breasts; she was posed as a farm girl, lying spread-legged in a haystack. Hoa knew it must be true that they had such girls in America, and why Bill didn't want one of these goddesses, that was a mystery.

She wanted something to look at. She had picked up the paperback books that were scattered around, and stacked them neatly near the big pile of C-ration cases. She had hoped to find one of them interesting, but American books had no pictures in them, for some reason, and she could not understand even the titles. She had stacked his magazines, too, but didn't want to open one, since they would be filled with pictures of naked girls, and even the leanest of them had a body that could put her to shame.

She closed the locker door, went to Bill's refrigerator, squatted and opened it, caught the soda and beer cans that spilled out. She reached for the crackers and the can of cheese that came out in a ribbon.

She had her hands full: the crackers, the cheese, and a can of 7-Up, and she went to the bunk, sat on it, used the footlocker for a table, opened the can of soda wishing she had tea. A sip of the soda and it was too sweet. The crackers were soggy but the cheese was not bad, although of course she was no expert on cheese.

She ate and looked around the room. Definitely it was not Vietnamese. What Vietnamese home had all these things? Bill was a sergeant of the lowest rank, and yet he had the refrigerator, a small toaster oven, the shortwave radio, two Sanyo fans. He even had, in the bottom of his footlocker, the strangest electric thing Hoa had ever seen. She was ashamed of herself for being so nosy, and looking so deeply into Bill's locker; but she'd had little to do all day.

Once again, she opened the footlocker and drew out the strange thing. Still eating the crackers and cheese, she pushed the box and can aside to make room.

The strange thing was a rusty tin rectangle, green with a border of red. The green part was laid out with white stripes, and looked like a miniature soccer field. There were lots of little plastic men-figures, lying on their sides, half of them yellow and half of them red, and there was a steel man, too, bigger than the rest. Hoa stood a few of the men up. She could not figure it out exactly. They must be different teams, as in soccer. Then she noticed the little steel goalposts that folded up. That, too, was like soccer. But what was the method of this game? She stood up all the men-figures and tried to study it out.

The only way to find out was to plug it in, she decided. She stood, closed the box of crackers, drank all she could take of the soda, a tiny sip. An electric cord came out of the game, and she plugged it in. Nothing happened.

There was a switch on the cord. She sat on the bed, nervous, then looked away and threw the switch. A loud humming sound startled her, and the tin field shook, and the little men-figures moved at random, running into each other and pushing each other down, some of them going in circles and some of them going straight.

She laughed. A game that played all by itself! She watched, fascinated; in a few moments all the little men-figures had fallen down.

She heard Bill's footsteps coming down the long corridor. Some instinct made her turn the game off, and try to shove it under the bed, but Bill opened the door and caught her squatting with the game in her hands; he didn't seem to notice it.

"Got guard all night," Bill said. He put his rifle down on the bunk. "I want you with me." His face was tight, his voice steely and nervous. "Bring your jacket, it's going to be cold."

She let the game stay on the floor, stood and put her arms around him.

He rubbed her on the back. He wasn't angry at her! "Have you ever fired a rifle?"

She shook her head.

"Never?"

"Never," she said.

"Do you think you could?"

"I do not think so," she said.

"We'll find out," he said. "Come on."

He let go of her, opened his wall locker and took out two packs of Luckies, put his hand on a bourbon bottle but then left it, closed the door on it. She went to her bundle, untied the knot, took out the cloth jacket she had bought years ago, on a school trip to Can Tho, then wrapped up in a black shawl that had been her mother's.

"Going to be warm enough?" He took his field jacket off a hook on the back of the door, picked up his rifle. "You sure?"

She nodded and followed him out of the barracks and into the night. They walked along metal planking and over a ditch, then out to the asphalt road. Bill walked fast, with long-legged strides.

The base was dark except for the perimeter lights, big banks of them on poles; they walked toward those lights

and were getting there quickly. Bill walked so fast that
Hoa had to run to keep up; the road turned to sand under
her feet when they got near the river. The guard towers
were spaced out, perhaps a hundred meters from each
other. They were set back from the lights and even up
close, Hoa could not tell whether the dark lumps inside
were Arvin boys or American dummies.

At one tower Bill went underneath, in total darkness,
and she could hear him climbing the ladder, pushing
through the trapdoor; then he called her name. She went
under there and felt for the ladder. He took her under the
arms and pulled her up.

She looked over the wall at a night view of the river she
had never seen; it was bright, light reflected in many pinpoints from the surface of the water. In between the river
and the tower was a wide strip of sand, and three barbed-
wire fences, with rolls of concertina wire squiggled between them. There were claymore mines down there,
three electric wires came up and over the wall, ending in
green plastic detonators. Bill or someone had filled the
tower with weapons and ammunition and equipment, and
most of it was on the walls, dimly visible: a big military
radio with a microphone attached, two black machine
guns trailing hundreds of linked brass bullets, a grenade
launcher, an M-16 rifle, cloth belts filled with bullet clips,
aluminum tubes containing parachute flares, and at least a
dozen hand grenades. Bill was fooling with one machine
gun, opening the lid and pulling on the ammo belt.

She watched him. He was cursing softly, and nervous
with his hands. It made her look away, past the two dummies and at the river, with its lily pads floating to the sea.
The ones that didn't make it would come floating all the
way back at the change of tide, and that thought gave Hoa
a nervous stomach.

"We're going to have a little target practice," Bill said.
He was at the machine gun. "Come here."

She shook her head. "I cannot shoot that."

"You might have to."

"It is too big for me."

"Damn it," Bill said, so loud that it scared her. He came toward her and put an M-16 rifle in her hand. She had never held one before. It was so light!

"It's very easy," said Bill. "Just pull the trigger, and when it's done shooting"—he guided her finger to a button—"press that, the clip will drop out, and you shove a fresh one it. All there is to it. Okay? Let's try it now."

He led her to the wall. "Keep down except for your head and shoulders. Okay?" He brought her arms up with the gun in them, forced the points of her elbows down on top of the wall. It hurt! "Use the wall to steady yourself." But still she was shaking. She sighted down the rifle as she had seen soldiers do.

"Okay, one more thing," Bill said. "This switch goes like this. Feel it." He brought her fingers to it. "Safety, single shot, automatic. Do it." She moved the switch back and forth. "Single shot. Okay? Now take aim."

"Where?"

"That house over there." He pointed at the white stone house that had been so blasted apart that only some of the walls were standing. She had it in her shaky sights.

"It is someone's house," Hoa said.

"Nobody lives there—now squeeze off a round."

"Still, it is someone's house. I know the family that once lived in that house."

"Shoot it," Bill said. She looked at him, hard. "Don't take your eyes off the target. Fire!" he said. She looked down the sight, held two fingers sweaty on the trigger—the gun went off! Hoa gave a short scream.

"I think you hit it," Bill said. "Fire three rounds." She sighted, less shaky now, and pulled the trigger once, then twice quickly.

"You've got it," Bill said. "Automatic."

He flicked the switch for her. "Just hold the trigger back and let it go."

She held the trigger back and the gun jumped around in her arms and red streaks came out like they were coming from her eyes and some struck the water, some hit the house, and some went in wild arcs; when she was finished, she felt stinging on her feet; hot casings had landed there. She stepped away from them. Bill put a new clip in her rifle.

"What have your heard today?" Hoa said. "News."

"It's going to be tight for a couple of days." He put his hand on her shoulder.

"They are not coming for the Delta?"

"Not so far," he said.

"What about your idea to run away?"

"I'm taking care of it," Bill said. "But we've got to wait five days. Until payday."

"Why?"

"Because it takes money, Hoa, and I don't have a nickel on me."

It was almost first light when Lemmen started to relax. He knew dawn was near without looking at the sky, without checking his watch; he had been awake for hundreds of dawns. He knew it by the smell of things, by the flow of the river, and most of all, by the quiet.

He had disassembled the dummy Dick, and freed the lawn chair, and now he sat back in it, almost ready to sleep. He sat with his carbine in his lap, looking upriver at the gray hazy shadows; the sun was beginning to rise at his back. He kept thinking of breakfast. He had brought every kind of weapon out here, but had forgotten food. Well, they would open some C-ration ham and eggs back in his room, have some crackers and bread and C-ration coffee. He looked at Hoa, asleep in the hammock, her long curls hanging through the net. She was huddled into herself.

She had taken most of the night's guard. Lemmen needed the sleep—he would be on duty all day again, at the main gate. That's how angry Command was, to put him on twenty-four-hour duty. But Lemmen hoped that such harshness might work for him. Maybe Command would feel guilty, after a few days, and rip up the orders for Fort Carson.

He lit a cigarette—that would keep the breakfast pangs away. He thought about his plan. Which had been inspired, actually, by Nuong and by the river, and by the lily pad clusters floating to the sea. If Nuong could buy his family aboard a trawler, there must be hundreds of boats out there, the captains picking up refugees and making a fortune. On payday, Lemmen would come into possession of $362. Which might or might not be enough; Nuong had said the passage was $120. But was that for one person or four? Lemmen did not know how much money Nuong actually took with him—it could have been a thousand. He didn't know if Nuong actually made it—he'd said the price was going up every day. Every day might be my last chance, Lemmen thought. If he and Hoa could steal a sampan, they'd get to the coast in a few hours.

One thing that still bothered him was the thought of Van. He would feel better if he could bring that boy with him. To hell with an orphanage, he should get that kid out of this country. But how could he bring the boy out of the swamp? Only by bribing the Dai-ui. How could he manage that? There was no way to the swamp except by helicopter, unless you knew the river. And what if he took Van with him but didn't have enough money to get three people onto a boat?

He stood, took a last drag of his cigarette, pitched it toward the river. Put his hand on the black barrel of the machine gun, wicked off the morning dew. He decided to take one of these guns back to his room; in the romantic part of his brain he saw himself and Hoa, just the two of them, shooting down attackers, him firing, Hoa feeding, a last stand, like some black-and-white movie. That was ridiculous, but it really wouldn't hurt to have a machine gun in the room—even though the radio had been quiet all night, not a single attack reported in the Delta.

He looked upriver; out of boredom he used the day's first light to sight the machine gun down the left bank, and that was when he saw dark dots. He realized they must be boats. There were a lot of them, coming in silence, as fast as the flow of the river. Lemmen felt his throat tighten, he bent to the floor for the claymore clackers, dropped them on top of the wall.

The boats came around the final twist of the river. Lemmen started talking to himself as he straightened the cotter pins in grenade after grenade, dropped them next to the clackers. Save the claymores for last, he told himself. Keep down below the wall. Wake Hoa. Have her feed the machine gun. Call a mayday on the radio.

But he couldn't move, or talk, or do anything. The boats were coming, and he saw people in the boats, soldiers in uniform. Maybe a dozen boats in all.

What he wanted desperately to hear was Cobra engines starting—he glanced at the runway, but of course there weren't any airworthy Cobras left, or anybody to fly them, and he looked back at the boats and raised the sights of the machine gun. He croaked out Hoa's name, and she scrambled out of the hammock. The flotilla was coming out from dark, tree-lined banks and into the gray light.

Hoa was next to him—he pushed her down behind the wall. Motioned to a can of machine-gun ammo. "Open it" was all he could get out, and her fingers fumbled at the latches.

The first sampan floated out from the shadows, and Lemmen could almost see faces, it was jammed with soldiers and weapons. Lemmen leaned his shoulder into the stock of the machine gun, grabbed it under the barrel, squeezed the trigger. Arcs of red tracer zipped out, he didn't hear any noise, just red arcs splashing into the river short of the front sampan, soldiers diving over the sides of all the boats; Lemmen let up on the trigger, raised the barrel, soldiers were swimming everywhere, he held the trigger back again, the gun bounced in his hands, he was only aware of the brass shells falling around his boots and the heads and shoulders in the river and the empty sampans—then a shout in his ear and Hoa's arms around his neck. "No! Stop!"

Lemmen brought his elbow up to knock Hoa away, then saw something happen in the river: A soldier swam to the front sampan, reached in, brought out a white cloth on a stick. The people in the river floated toward the tower along with empty boats and a scattered mess of packs and bundles, and Lemmen suddenly saw women out there, and a few children too. It took him maybe two full seconds to realize that these people weren't NVA but escaping Arvins—it came to him finally like a shock of electricity, and when he looked around, Hoa was already scrambling down the ladder.

Lemmen followed her, out of the shadows under the tower, into the strip of sand along the banks. Hoa twisted and turned and bent and even crawled to get through the barbed wire, she set off a red tripflare, but kept going, the flare whooshed just in front of Lemmen's face. He stomped down on a roll of concertina, walked over it, razor edges tearing at his legs, his pants ripped, he let himself through the last fence, holding the top wire up, stepping on the bottom one, ducking through, beer cans rattling everywhere. He ran along the riverbank behind Hoa. Somebody in the river screamed. A sampan floated by empty, someone was still screaming—a boy's voice! Lemmen jumped into the river, up to his knees in water. People swam toward him. Where was the screaming coming from? Lemmen took two more steps into the slime, water to his thighs, almost fell forward, fought for balance, kept his left hand out toward a woman, who tried to angle in against the current, barely keeping water out of her mouth. He got her by the wrist, pulled her in, pushed her up on the bank. He'd lost track of Hoa. He saw a hand come up from the water, a small hand, he ripped off his shirt and dived.

He splashed hard, using the current for speed, and caught up with a sampan. He guided it along, kicking. Glanced back, he was already a long way from the bank. There was Hoa, up to her waist in water, pulling people in. He saw a form under the surface just ahead of him, let go of the sampan, gulped air, dived, kicked down, reached out, in the murky water he could see only gray, he grabbed hair, grabbed a collar, kicked for the surface, broke water, brought a small somebody with him, kicked to keep them afloat, kicked for the sampan, towing this half-conscious thing, chin in the crook of his arm, he got one hand on the stern of the sampan, grabbed it, groaned with relief, looked down at the face, it wasn't Van! The face was too old, too fat, too gray, swollen around the mouth—the Dai-ui! Lemmen tilted the sampan, slapped the man's hands on its edge. "You hear me? Hang on."

The Dai-ui seemed to be hanging on all right. They were in the middle of the river, in a swirling current, the sampan sweeping sideways. They were getting farther and farther from the other people, who were swimming toward Hoa on the bank, pushing and hanging on to their sampans, packs, bundles. The barbed wire and towers of Delta Town seemed very high, and Lemmen looked at a tower, hoping no nervous Arvin teenager was ready to fire.

He looked upriver for Van. A vision of Jimmy Carney came to his mind, floating bloated and purple in this same part of the river, and Lemmen hoisted and kicked himself into the sampan, picked up an oar from the bottom, glanced to see that the Dai-ui was hanging on, he was going to row upstream and find Van no matter what; then he saw the boy, sitting high on the bank and waving.

At sundown, the Dai-ui came with two young soldiers to relieve Lemmen at the gate. Lemmen slouched, exhausted, as the soldiers took standing positions facing the crowd on the other side. His replacements were boys hardly five feet tall, dressed in ill-fitting clothes, holding M-16s. They got a quick lecture from the Dai-ui, made their faces hard, and pointed those rifles at the crowd. Pushed up against the gate, women, old men, and children had their fingers wrapped in the wire. The shouting and shoving of the morning had gradually become silence. The Dai-ui walked behind the soldiers and said something sharp and nasty to them. He had lost his whipping stick in the river, so as punctuation to his commands, he kicked each soldier in the ass, and their faces flinched and became set again, grim and hard.

Lemmen was glad to get away, but as he turned his back and started walking, people cried out, some of them yelling, "GI." The shouts made Lemmen feel numb, but his feet kept him moving with the Dai-ui. Over the course of the day's guard, he'd thought he recognized a few faces;

the people in the front line had constantly changed, some giving up and joining the crowd walking north along the highway, others taking their places, faces and fingers pressed to the gate. He thought he might have seen that old man from Hoa's village, and a girl who years ago had worked at the mess hall; once, he was almost sure, in the back of the crowd, he saw Ba, that gray-haired lady who ran the Hello and Goodbye in the old days. The mess hall girl had carried a baby, a tiny thing that looked like a newborn, with skin like rubber and the thinnest kind of hair; the baby's arms had been locked around the mother's neck. The woman had shouted something and pointed to her baby; Lemmen didn't understand the words.

"We can't just let them in, can we?" Lemmen said. Then he remembered that the Dai-ui spoke no English. The Dai-ui, walking beside him, shrugged. He had swollen lips and a big gap in his mouth where his gold teeth had been kicked out. "They're safer out there," Lemmen said, "and besides, we don't have enough food for all of them." He tried to get something of that across to the Dai-ui; he rubbed his stomach and pointed to his mouth. The Dai-ui nodded, lifted two fingers like chopsticks, and put them near his mouth.

They passed Command's trailer, a light was already burning. They walked in front of the cavalry mural and around to the door of Lemmen's barracks. When the Dai-ui opened the door, Lemmen was astonished; the barracks had been taken over—it was full of people, squatting, talking, playing cards; rifles, packs, and ammunition lay on the floor and the bunks. Someone had set a Cao Dai altar near Lemmen's room, with a cloth banner depicting that single eye in a pyramid, and little statues of the helper gods, all bathed in the light of a blue lantern. Children slept in bunks and on footlockers; women were gathered in the rear talking and sewing.

Lemmen recognized nobody. It wasn't until he got within a few steps of his room that he realized how tired and sleepy he was. He glanced back; the Dai-ui had stopped to talk to a woman sewing a uniform.

He opened his door and found Hoa listening to two radios, the shortwave and the military. The military was all static with an occasional squeal. Out of the shortwave came the voice of Ho Chi Minnie. Lemmen sat on his bunk, too exhausted to greet Hoa or even listen to the radio. The Dai-ui was in the doorway saying something to Hoa as Lemmen collapsed backward, then closed his eyes. He heard Hoa call his name.

"Bill, he says he is hungry," she said.

"Oh," Lemmen said. He did not open his eyes.

"He says you should give him some of your food."

"Give him all of it," Lemmen said. His voice sounded tired even to him. His eyes still closed, he heard the Dai-ui saying something, then the scrape of C-ration cases being dragged across the floor. From the other side of the plywood wall came light footsteps, people murmuring and talking. The door closed on those sounds, and Lemmen dropped into a sleep.

It was a hell of a sleep, with a dozen dreams. Everything jumbled into one. Nothing came out right. Van a grown-up soldier in uniform; the Dai-ui rich and comfortable, red star on his hat, running a platoon of red-uniformed soldiers; Nuong in a labor camp, his family drowned; Command retired in Florida, Worthington alive and drunk in the Philippines; and behind it all, the thump of mortars and clattering of machine guns and the shouting of battle and the screaming of the Seven Sisters and the pop-pop sound of choppers coming in and Carney lying in a deep skag sleep in his bunk and a dead VC scout covered with flies who sat up and talked in a friendly way, complimenting Lemmen on a job well done, and Holloway sitting in the Hello and Goodbye with two girls squeezed in his lap, then Hoa saying "Bill" into his ear.

He opened his eyes.

"Bill!"

The two lights of the radio dimly lit the room. Hoa's face in outline. Her hand on his shoulder.

He bolted straight, grabbed his carbine, jumped out of bed. He was all sweat.

"Listen!"

He held Sam in unsteady hands. Expected to hear the thump of mortars or the whoosh of rockets, but there was only a woman's voice.

"Too many," the voice said, "too many times we have warned you that the end is near, and now you will believe us. In our great victory the people are welcoming our soldiers with open arms, and once again we say to traitors and foreigners, you have this chance to leave and let the river of history roll on its Vietnamese way."

"She says they are going toward Little America," Hoa said. "She says in Saigon they are screaming in panic."

Bill reached over and shut Ho Chi Minnie off. "What's on the military band?"

"Nothing," Hoa said. "Silence."

"Can Tho?"

"Silence."

"No calls for help?"

"Silence! I am worried about my brother."

"Okay," Lemmen said. "Okay, let me think."

"The woman says there are big attacks in the north," Hoa said. "But on Saigon radio they say it is not true, and there is only normal fighting."

Lemmen didn't know what to think. His eyes and throat were scratchy, his stomach hollow from hunger. Slowly, he sat down on the edge of the bunk.

The plywood door crept open. At half its height Lemmen saw a face—Van, an unlit cigarette stuck in his mouth.

"Okay!" the boy said, and grinned.

"Get in here," Lemmen said. *"Lai day."*

The boy came in. He was bare-chested, wearing Arvin

uniform pants so long that the bottoms made shoes for his feet, dragged on the concrete floor.

"Call in the Dai-ui," Lemmen said to Hoa. She went out the door, and Lemmen watched her go, then grabbed Van by one wrist. "You stay with me."

"No *bic*," the boy said, the cigarette moving in his mouth.

"Sit down," Lemmen said, and pushed him onto the footlocker. "Have you got a cigarette for me?" Lemmen said. When the boy shrugged his shoulders, Lemmen said: "Salem me." Van grinned and went into his deep pockets, came out with a tiny pack of Winstons. Lemmen took one and searched his own pockets for his lighter. Lit his, lit Van's. The boy puffed without inhaling, blew out a roundish cloud of smoke. "Number one!" he said.

The Dai-ui came in, Hoa behind him. She shut the door and stood against it, hands behind her back.

"We've got fifty dollars for you," Lemmen said. "American."

Hoa translated and the Dai-ui smiled in a swollen, painful way.

"We don't want this boy to become a soldier. We want you to release him to our custody," Lemmen said. "We'll put him in an orphanage in Saigon."

Hoa translated that, and the Dai-ui's smile got broader, more pained. He looked at Van, looked down and shuffled his boots, then shifted his eyes sideways at Hoa and made some reply.

"He cannot," Hoa said. "He is like a father."

Lemmen thought for a minute. "Nuong told me this boy was an orphan."

Hoa translated and said, "Bill, you do not understand, under custom, this boy belongs to the Dai-ui."

"How much?" Bill said.

Hoa talked to the Dai-ui, who smiled at her, showing the black hole in his mouth, then said something very short and precise, then rubbed his mouth and said something longer. Hoa gave him a stern and disgusted look, then turned to Bill and said: "He said, do you remember when he had gold teeth? He said the United States owes him one thousand dollars."

The Fishwomen
Whisper

"Sir," Lemmen said. His boonie hat in his hand, he stood at the doorway of Command's trailer in the sweat-breaking heat of nine in the morning. He'd just come from another night on tower guard; he hadn't washed since Little America, except for the dunking in the Mekong. He could smell himself, and felt covered with grit.

"Sir?" Lemmen said, louder. He stepped in and closed the door. In the main rooms there was no one: dirty dishes spread over the table, laundry piled in one corner.

"Sir!" Lemmen shouted.

"What in goddamn . . ." Command said, his face at the door of the inner room. "Well, come the hell in, Lemmen, don't stand around." Command disappeared and left the door open.

Inside, a miniature air conditioner was whirring full blast. Command sat at a desk with his back to Lemmen, looking over folders he'd pulled out of a file cabinet. His gray hair was combed neatly back and he wore a blue rayon shirt, khaki slacks, loafers. Above his head was a huge map; it showed only the lower parts of the country and said *Mouths of the Mekong*. Lemmen studied it, tried to get some idea of its scale. Two and a half inches from Vinh Long to the South China Sea. How far was that, really? He guessed: twenty-five miles.

"God damn those Saigon . . ." Command said, without turning to look at Lemmen. He kept groping for a word. "Cowards, that's what they are, Lemmen."

Lemmen walked around to the edge of the table, where he could at least see Command's face. Which looked small. Command was a small man, and Lemmen just realized that, seeing him out of uniform.

"Rumor I hear is, Saigon's thinking about giving up the whole goddamn highlands. The whole of it! You know how hard the cav fought for those highlands?" He looked directly at Lemmen for the first time. "We got our B-52s flying though. Ain't going to give Charley this one easy. What are you standing for? Sit down."

There wasn't a chair, but Lemmen found a seat on a stack of luggage.

"You see anything on the river last night?"

"No, sir," Lemmen said.

"Didn't think so. I think we've been outscarecrowed." He pointed at the map, at the red line of the Cambodian border. "They probably got two cooks, a chaplain, and a bottle washer out there. Every Charley in the world is in the highlands right now." He rapped his knuckles on the wall, where the highlands would be if only the map went that far. "Just when we were looking the other way."

"What's the news from the U.S. command, sir?"

"The news?" Command said, and turned on him, as if any bad news would be his fault. "The news is, they're drawing a line just south of Ban Me Thuot, and that's going to be the new republic. That and a little bit of coast-line." His lips curled back. "Lucky if it lasts a year."

"I came to ask you a favor, sir, although I know I don't deserve it."

"You're damn right you don't deserve it," Command

said, and turned his wooden swivel chair to face Lemmen squarely.

"I wondered if I could get an advance on my pay, sir."

"An advance!" Command shouted.

"Yes sir. I need fifteen hundred dollars, sir."

Command rolled his eyeballs. "Well, Lemmen, what kind of payroll do you think I've got down here? There's just me and you. Way things are going, we'll be lucky to get paid at all. I'm not even sure how long Route Four's going to be open. What the hell do you need fifteen hundred dollars for?"

"Personal," Lemmen said.

"Personal!"

"It's very personal, sir."

Command reached into the file cabinet, brought out a small, unlocked cashbox, opened it; Lemmen could see a few twenties. "I've got about two hundred dollars in petty cash, Sergeant. Now isn't that pathetic? A major in the greatest calvary ever rode a horse, and he has two hundred measly dollars in cash." Command waved his hand. "I couldn't give you the kind of advance you want, even if I had it. See the Red Cross."

"Sir, the Red Cross is in Saigon."

"I know damn well the Red Cross is in Saigon, Sergeant."

"Well, how can I get up there, sir?"

"You can't right now. My advice is to wait it out—whatever your personal needs are. Hell, we all have personal needs." He wheeled his chair to the file cabinet, pulled a wastebasket from under the table. Reached over to open the cabinet, took whole sections from its drawers, dropped them into the wastebasket. "You got a light on you, Lemmen?"

Lemmen fumbled for his lighter, handed it over.

"I don't have the luxury of a paper shredder," Command said, and started a fire in the basket. "One thing's sure, Charley's going to have a hell of time reading that.

Oh, he'd love to get his hands on it. List of every one of the Little People who's ever worked for the Ninth Cav."

"Burn it good, sir."

"I intend to, Lemmen." He watched the flames lick over the edge of the basket. "Destroying my whole command," he said. "Everything." He pushed his chair back from the table. "Get some sleep today. The Arvins can handle the gate. At last light I want you out in the towers, showing those boys the ropes. It's their show now. And God help 'em."

He turned his head to check the flames, reached into the files for more paper. "You heard anything about Sergeant Nuong?"

"No, sir. I lent him a little money, that's why I'm broke."

Command dropped the paper into the flames. "Well, he's a goner. If he's smart."

"So am I, sir."

"What?"

"Going to sleep."

"Well, you go ahead, Lemmen," Command said. "You're going to need all the shut-eye you can get."

Lemmen backed out the door. He still had his hat in his hand, hadn't gotten what he had come for, and there was no one besides Command who could give it to him. That was the military, they gave you food, clothing, shelter, transportation, everything, but you paid a price. You were a slave to the guy above you, followed his orders without question—that was the deal. He walked through the messy kitchen and out into the heat of the sun.

On his way around the barracks he passed the mural: those blue-uniformed soldiers from another century, that Arizona landscape, the scrawled words *We're Not Here.* The mural looked different; if he glanced at it sideways, the soldiers seemed to be moving. He was seeing things, lack of sleep. He faced the painting squarely. Those soldiers looked lonely, just a few of them in that hostile landscape;

the Indians must have been everywhere, watching them. They were probably frightened and, God knows, tired. One soldier was standing while the others were crouched around the fire. That standing soldier had his back to the others as he stared at the hills. Was he scouting those hills for signs of the enemy? Or was he thinking of hopping on his horse and getting the hell out of there? Was he dreaming of an easy life, señoritas and tequila in Mexico?

Lemmen went around to the front of the barracks and sat on the one concrete step to do some thinking.

What if they lost the war? It didn't seem really possible, but even Command said Saigon might not last. They were giving up the highlands. It was time to decide. He'd been here less than two years total but it seemed like so much of his life. How could he save any of it? Only one solution he could think of. It was a traitor's solution, but it stuck with him anyway. His only way out. He would become a thief and maybe even a murderer, but what difference did that make now? He would steal Command's two hundred dollars. He would take Van away from the Dai-ui at gunpoint. Shoot the Dai-ui if he had to. Take Hoa and Van and they would leave in one of those sampans that the Post Twelve soldiers had brought downriver. Lemmen would bring money, booze, cigarettes, Nuong's jewelry, whatever he could steal from Command or anywhere that would help barter them aboard a boat. They would take their chance on the river. Twenty-five miles to the sea!

It was getting near sundown and Hoa knew she would
have to wake him. Which was too bad—he was so tired,
and in his so-called sleep he had squirmed for hours, sometimes waking to mumble words, but nothing Hoa could
understand. She touched him on the chest. He had not
taken off his uniform—not even his boots. She whispered
his name. He grunted.

She sat down on the footlocker just to watch him. On
either side of her were fans blowing directly on Bill, to
cool him in his sleep. She wondered about his crazy plan.
Suppose the VC were along the river? Suppose they
floated down to the ocean and there were no boats to pick
them up? The idea of the ocean frightened Hoa, it must be
so rough, with giant waves that would overturn a sampan
in a flash. Even if they managed to get on a boat, how
could they be sure the captain was not a pirate? And what
was it like in Manila, and how would they get so far away,
and what would they do there? Perhaps they would have
to live in an alley and starve. That thought reminded Hoa
of her mother, alone in the capital, without a daughter or

son to look out for her; she thought of her brother in Can Tho, who would be furious, if he had chanced a ride on Route 4, to find their home empty. She thought about how she had failed her family, that was certain, and how they owed her nothing now. Except, of course, her mother would forgive her anything, although the forgiveness might take a while.

She was restless and felt kept, like a chicken in a coop. She had been in this room for days; once when she tried to go out and join the gossiping Arvin wives, they had turned cold backs on her and pretended not to hear or see her, and soon she realized that in their eyes, she was a whore for the Americans. So she'd come back to the room, with only the radio to entertain her. But the shortwave broadcasts were hardly entertaining: Ho Chi Minnie; lying newscasts from Saigon; horrible rumors from Cambodia. She mostly listened to the American station, which at least played music.

"Bill," she said, and pushed him on the shoulder. He opened his eyes. They were bloodshot but he had not been drinking. He did not smell nice but she did not care. In some ways she liked his smell, which was more like a peasant's, and different from Vietnamese city men's—they smelled of hair tonic and perfume.

He stared at her, not quite awake.

"It is almost time," she said.

He rolled onto his side. From his pocket he drew a watch. It was tangled with a gold chain holding a cross with the god Jesus on it. He said, "Four-thirty," with a moan and dropped his head on the pillow.

She got into bed with him, snuggled up to his body. She undid two of his shirt buttons. How could he stay buttoned up in this heat? She put her hand on his chest, then realized she was getting sexy ideas.

"Bill," she said. "Do you want to make love?"

"What?"

"Make love to me."

He breathed out very hard.

Why? Hoa asked herself. Was this a chore? She bit her lip. "Here," she said, and undid the top button of her blouse. No bra was in the way of her breasts. She undid another button, took off her blouse, folded it, and lay back on the bunk; she felt like a whore-mother, her breasts tingling in the cool of the fan air. Bill stood to undress. She pushed off her black trousers and underpants all at once, down past her knees, off her ankles, folded them on the footlocker, and lay back again. Beads of sweat cooled on her pubic hairs; it felt very nice. From the other side of the plywood wall she could hear the Arvin wives gossiping; they would hear their lovemaking, and for once Hoa didn't care.

Bill came back into bed, and she closed her eyes. She felt his fingers on her cheek, his lips on her face, his lips on her lips; she let one leg spread out on the bunk, then felt his lips coming down gently on her throat, down her bony parts and to her breasts, he took her whole breast into his mouth, played it with his tongue, let it out, then sucked the other one; his hard thing she could feel on her thigh, then he licked with his wet tongue down to her belly button and once, twice down each leg, then went between her with his tongue, around and around. In a minute, the tremendous weight of him came on top of her and slowly and carefully, teasing, he slipped inside her. Her arms went around his neck and she breathed slow and deep.

She had her eyes closed for a long time. In her mind she was nowhere near this room. In her mind she saw in lingering scenes the schoolboy Thuoi, riding his rusty bike alongside as she walked down the path home; Thuoi riding and teasing her about her curly hair, and calling her first-place girl in a taunting way, because she had won a ribbon in language class; Thuoi calling her smarty and skinny-bones day after day and as it turned out, he'd only wanted to make love to her, as he proved one sundown when he took her and a bottle of French wine to a patch of

grass between the soccer field and the rice warehouse; Hoa
could smell that grass now, that grass and the musty
mounds of drying rice, and the wine and cigarettes on
Thuoi's breath. In her mind she saw herself walking down
that same path from the highway, alone, after Thuoi had
gone to Saigon to become an engineer, after he had been
drafted during his first year in college, after he had been
sent to Quang Tri as a lieutenant, after his foot had been
blown off at the ankle and his whole body punctured with
shrapnel and he had returned to Saigon, in and out of
hospitals with infections and with drinking until he died
of pneumonia. From then, Hoa walked down the path
alone until the day she went to work for Ba the bar-
mother.

In her mind she saw Liu, the soldier boy who stopped in
with GIs day after day; he pretended to like those GIs but
only wanted to buy and trade things—Liu, a skinny, mus-
cular Saigon boy, who flirted with her, made kissing lips
at her; at first she ignored him and could not believe a
Saigon boy would like her, but then she found herself
thinking about him with a certain warm feeling; and one
night, as if he could read her heart, he snuck around the
back to call at Hoa's window, climbed into her bed, and
kissed her and screwed her very hard. Liu did this three
nights in a row and then acted as if he owned her, Liu
with his one gold tooth in his mouth, Liu who had memo-
rized romantic poetry in French—Victor Hugo poetry—
and recited it for her, Liu who talked of taking her to the
city, Liu the liar who said he loved her and had been coming to the bar for weeks just to watch her. On the third
and last night he screwed her, Liu demanded that she quit
her job, and when she refused, he called her a filthy GI
cocksucker. On that monsoon night he slapped her hard, a
sound that brought Ba out of bed and running for Hoa's
room, which resulted in Liu going out the window in his
underpants. That was the last she saw of him, his ass in

the window, slithering out into the rain, his feet thumping on the dock below.

In her mind Hoa was alone for a thousand nights in her bedroll in the back room of the Hello and Goodbye; every afternoon and evening spent surrounded by crude foreign boys, and most nights alone, sometimes black-and-blue in the places they had pinched her. Ba was strict in keeping her promise to Hoa's mother—no GIs in the girls' rooms. Of course Hoa, like the other girls, had sometimes made an exception, for clean and nice boys with money who would promise to be fast and quiet, but she could not remember any of them now—mostly she saw herself alone, pressing against the cinder block wall for coolness in the night, listening to the sounds of Ba padding the halls to check on the girls. Hoa remembered listening to the water lap against the dock, listening to the sampans clunk each other and creak with the movement of the river.

Hoa held on tight to Bill. She imagined waking up next to him in California, where there were cool mountains and people could see the blue ocean from their homes. Her ideas were all pastel colors and clean towns and ocean breeze. Hoa felt a whirling dizziness, her mind went utterly empty of images, a white hum all around her and Bill suddenly grabbed her as tight as a clamp, shuddered, and came down heavy. She was aware that they were sweating, making small noises, naked on a bunk in a darkening room. Bill was kissing every part of her face. He was also nearly crushing her to death.

"You are hurting me," she said.

"I want to take you with me, everywhere I go," Bill said into her ear.

"You are hurting me," she said.

"I'm not going to let you go, Hoa," he said. Was he even hearing her?

"Please," she said.

"We're going to find somewhere nice to live," he said.

"Bill!" she said. She could barely breathe. She wriggled and pushed.

"Don't push me away, Hoa."

"You are hurting me!" she said.

He pushed his weight up on his elbows.

"Thank you," she said. She could breathe!

"You should have told me," he said.

"You crushed my ribs," she said.

"Sorry," he said. He began to push himself off her and Hoa grabbed at his sides, pulled him down.

"Don't go away," she said. "I like you here."

He kissed her on the nose, the eyes, the cheeks.

"I like that," she said. Her hands went to his chest, shoulders, neck, arm muscles, to feel how strong he was.

"I'm sorry I hurt you," he said.

"I feel much better now," she said.

"Me too," he said. She laughed. He pushed himself away and this time her arms could not hold him. He stood, took both her ankles in one hand, lifted her legs, sat down on the bunk, put her legs over his lap. Moved his hand all the way up her thigh and teased her middle hair, then took her hand. "Do you love me?" he asked.

"Of course," she said.

"Honestly?" he said. He was looking hard into her eyes.

"Yes, I do," she said. "I would not fuck you unless I love you."

"It's not polite to say it that way."

"I don't care."

He squeezed her hand. He for some reason looked around the room, as if someone might be listening. He said: "You ought to be ready to leave any time. I hope you love me, *men oy*, because we could be stuck with each other for a long, long time."

It was dark and Lemmen was late, but what did it matter? What was Command going to do to him now? Just maybe, he thought, these were the last orders he'd ever follow, from Command or anyone else. He leaned against the mural in the dark. To steady himself against a dizzy feeling, and to wait for Hoa and the Dai-ui. Need more sleep, he told himself. Need to eat better. Need a lot of strength for tomorrow night, the date of departure set firmly in his mind.

He stretched to his tiptoes and looked in the screen window for Hoa. But what he saw, in the harsh light of the barracks, was Van. Van bare-chested and standing on a footlocker while one of the Arvin wives fussed at measuring and pinning Arvin trousers to fit him. Oh no, you don't, lady, Lemmen said to himself, you're not getting him in your army. I'm taking him with me.

He remembered his first day in-country, and that boy who'd thrown a rock at their bus. He had never gotten over the shock of that; he thought he had come here to help. To win a war. How ridiculous that was. It had taken him all this time to realize it. If he had been thinking, he would have known the moment that boy let go of the rock that he wasn't wanted here, was hurting the same people he was supposed to help. The people had spoken, right there with that rock! And what did some soldier in back of him say? "Welcome to Vietnam." It was all right in front of him if he'd only admitted that what he saw with his own eyes was true—and to hell with what he'd been told. What he was seeing with his own eyes now, that was true too—the look of the barracks. That told him something— that the Americans were through. The Arvins had lived in the barracks for two days, and it looked as if they had been there forever. They had put the mattresses on the floor, had divided the room with sheets hung from rafters, with women and boys at the back end, men up front. The Dai-ui squatted on the mattress farthest from the women, smoking, playing cards with his lieutenants, listening to a red radio—it was Lemmen's radio. It was playing Ho Chi Minnie, loud and clear.

Hoa came down the aisle and when she passed the Dai-ui, he said something to her; the other cardplayers glared at her, and the Dai-ui tossed down his cards, made some joke to the soldiers, a cigarette in his swollen lips, the long ash dropping off when he laughed. Then he got up and followed her.

They came out the door, Hoa first. The Dai-ui was dressed not for guard duty but in a white T-shirt and pink pants.

"The major wants me to show you your tower assignments," Lemmen said.

Hoa translated that. The Dai-ui stared at Lemmen, and, without breaking the stare, took the cigarette out of his lips and dropped it into the dirt, crushed it. He turned and barked a few commands into the open door of the barracks, the sound of his voice bouncing around the inside walls. He spit near Lemmen's feet, said the one English word Lemmen ever heard come from his lips: "Okay."

The Dai-ui shouted back more instructions, then the three of them walked without talking, down the asphalt road, passing the closed PX, the mortar pit that had no mortars, the empty ammo dump, the mud of the drained fire reservoir. In back of those things was a runway, still lit blue—but no aircraft had landed in days, and nothing on base was capable of taking off. They walked the sand road along the river, nobody saying a word in any language until they got to Tower Nine. Something—instinct—told Lemmen to look back, and trailing them was a small dark figure, and Lemmen knew just who it was.

"Up here," Lemmen said to the Dai-ui. He patted the ladder. The Dai-ui shrugged, so Lemmen went up first. He opened the trapdoor, hoisted himself in, put down a hand to help the Dai-ui, put down a hand to help Hoa.

There were two soldiers up there. They were boys and Lemmen did not recognize them, though for sure they had been out in the swamp last week, banging pots and pans. Well, Lemmen said to himself, they're all we've got now. He took a look downriver, realized that this was one of the most familiar places he'd ever been: right here in this tower, watching this river flow out of utter darkness and pass Delta Town, where for a couple of hundred yards it was lit by piercing arc lights, only to slip by in the dark again, and flow through the city and out to the sea. He wondered about the journey ahead of him. Neither he nor Hoa had been anywhere downriver. Maybe they should go to Saigon first. But that place was full of people trying to get out. They would be swamped by refugees. If only Worthington were alive; if only Nuong, by some miracle, were still in the city. He tried to push these thoughts out of his mind, and do his last duty.

"Do they know how to work this?" Lemmen asked, and put his hand out toward an M-60. "You *bic*?" he said to the boys; they grinned and nodded.

Lemmen felt a sudden surge of energy. "Each tower has a radio," he said, and touched it, "an M-60," he lifted the belt of bullets where it went into the machine gun's breech, "a grenade launcher." He pointed to the brown shotgunlike thing lying on the floor. "A supply of pop-flares and three or more claymores." He picked up a gray-green clacker and held it out for the Dai-ui to see. "Plus, of course, any personal weapons your men may want to bring up." Hoa's running translation reassured Lemmen. "The towers are sturdy," Lemmen said, and kicked the wall. "They can take a hit by anything right up to an RPG. There's a commanding view of the river, and, of course, all that barbed wire."

He gave Hoa time to catch up.

"Major Hopkins would like," Lemmen said, "for each of these towers to be manned twenty-four hours, with three of your best men, two of them awake at all times. Three"—he held up three fingers—"guards . . . do you understand?"

In a moment Hoa said: "They understand."

"It's a good fighting position," Lemmen said.

Hoa translated that, and the Dai-ui laughed. He said something to Hoa, who halfway smiled.

"He understands everything," she said.

"I hope the Dai-ui is not angry at me," Lemmen said. "I was not the one who kicked him off the helicopter. I had nothing to do with it. Tell him that."

Hoa translated and the Dai-ui listened, grinned. He gave a short answer.

"What did he say?" Lemmen asked.

"He says, 'bullshit,' " Hoa said.

The Dai-ui said something else, Hoa nodding.

"He says but he must thank you, because you left your radio with them, and from the radio they found out the truth."

"What truth?" Lemmen said.

Hoa translated and the Dai-ui wouldn't answer; he only looked at Lemmen and grinned. There was the pit-pat of someone coming up the ladder and Van's face appeared at the trapdoor hole. Van wriggled up, smiled, put out his hand for Lemmen to shake. "Okay, GI, okay you!" he said.

The boy circled behind Lemmen, avoiding the Dai-ui. His trousers fit nicely now, although he was still without a shirt. With one eye on the Dai-ui, he went around to the machine gun. He could barely see over the wall. He rubbed the black stock of the gun with one hand, then got behind it, tried to sight down it. Made a machine-gun noise in his teeth. "Number one," he said, and looked back at Lemmen, Hoa, the Dai-ui. "Number one. VC number ten."

The Dai-ui took one step, cuffed Van on the shoulder, growled a curse, pointed at the trapdoor. Van shrank toward it, going behind Lemmen again. There was a long string of cursing from the Dai-ui, and Van scrambled for the trapdoor, clambered down the ladder. For a few moments Lemmen watched the kid walk along the sand road. A boy's walk. Meandering. Stopping here and there at the side of the road. In and out of the light and shadow. Van stopped to inspect something, picked it up: a soda can. He reared back, threw the can toward the river, it fell short, with a *ping*, into the barbed wire.

The Dai-ui was talking and Hoa translated: "The Dai-ui wants to know about those houses." Lemmen looked across the river at the stone one, the bamboo one. They were half lit by Delta Town's arc lights.

"Tell him they're part of the free-fire zone," said Lemmen. "No one lives there."

Hoa translated that, listened to the Dai-ui, and told Lemmen: "No more questions. But the Dai-ui says, How about five hundred dollars for the boy?"

Lemmen glared at the Dai-ui, who made a shadowy, toothless smile. "Tell the Dai-ui fuck you," Lemmen said.

Hoa translated and the Dai-ui kept smiling. Lemmen climbed down the ladder, waited for her in the dark. "What did he say to that?" he asked when she came down.

"I only said we would like a lower price," Hoa said.

They walked along the river, careful to keep on the dark part of the road. Lemmen put his arm around her. "I was thinking about Sergeant Nuong," he said. "I hope he made it out all right, with his family."

He stopped and found himself staring across the river at those two houses. "You know what Nuong once told me? He said that stone house had been destroyed by its own strength, and the bamboo one stood because of its weakness. I could never figure that out."

"You were not here for that battle," Hoa said. "In the Tet, the VC hid behind the stone house, and the GIs shot it to pieces. But no one was foolish enough to hide behind bamboo."

Lemmen kept staring at those houses, found himself dreaming of a time he had never seen, a peaceful time when both houses would have been occupied by big families, when Delta Town was a field with a few cattle in it. His fantasy was disturbed by the flow of lily pads, their slow progress as they floated downriver. He tried to imagine how they would ever get to the sea traveling that slowly.

All they needed was a boat, a sampan, a raft—anything that would float. If the river moved at five miles an hour, then it was just a few hours to the sea. He watched a giant lily pad cluster snag on the far bank, then break free.

On the military radio, the Arvin Tower guards were talking in a sloppy, joking way—they were boys, not soldiers, and Lemmen sighed; he felt like going out there and giving them a dressing-down, whether they understood it or not. But no—he had to admit, somewhere, somehow, that he was through here.

He was sitting on the concrete floor, writing a note, using his footlocker for a desk. He watched Hoa, asleep, the in and out of her breathing. He got up for a moment, to take one finger and stroke each cheek. He had only a little time left and he wanted to explain it right, this, his last act as a military man. He crumpled the paper. Now he had only two sheets left, he'd have to work it over in his mind, just what to say.

He thought for a while then wrote quickly, a scribble. He wrote that he never imagined, in his worst nightmare, that he would end up a thief and a deserter. Sometimes you just have to break the rules—no, wrong, he scratched that out. Sometimes . . . things went wrong and you had no choice . . . but to do something . . . that went against everything you'd been trained for. *Sincerely,* he signed the note, *and with great regret, the former sergeant William Ernest Lemmen.*

One more sheet. Better to take a walk outside, Lemmen told himself, and think the wording over. He kissed Hoa's forehead. Shook out a Lucky. Walked out of his room, past the sleeping Vietnamese, and out into the clear night. In the distance he heard a sound that could have been thunder or could have been artillery. Lit his Lucky. Tried to imagine himself living by his wits, an outlaw, in Manila. How would he get by? Worthington could have done it.

It was hard to believe Worthington was really dead. Maybe it would have been easier, Lemmen thought, if he had seen some blood or at least gone to the funeral. Right now he needed Worthington. If Worthington had deserted to Manila, he would have ended up an advisor to Marcos! But Lemmen was no Worthington, he realized that now. How would he and Hoa live in a strange city? What did he know besides how to lead an ambush squad, how to fill out forms, the rote geometry of mortar fire? He could not be a pimp, he could not sell drugs—maybe he could change money. Maybe.

All he had to do was wait for Command to leave the trailer. Sooner or later the old man would come out, and Lemmen would take the money, any booze, jewelry—anything salable—and leave the note, and be gone by dawn.

Around the corner, a screen door shut, and in a moment a jeep engine started. Then headlights went on, like white knives in the night. Lemmen tried to get back in the shadow of the barracks but the headlights turned and came at him, stopped just short. Only when Lemmen went around to the side of the jeep could he see past the headlights, and of course it was Command driving.

"Sergeant, get on in here."

"Sir?"

"Get in."

Lemmen tossed his cigarette, took a seat in the jeep. He

looked in the back: Command's trophy case, broken down into three glass-front cabinets. The major put the gear-stick into first.

"At first light," Command said, "I've got be in Saigon. Don't ask me why. Orders are orders." He shifted into second gear. "So we're leaving, once and for all, Sergeant. That's confidential and unofficial, you understand, because officially, we've been out of here for years." The old man turned the jeep right, drove past his trailer, where one dull light shone from a window.

"Bastards," he said. "Oh, they're bastards, all of them." He kept driving.

"Charley, sir?"

"The bastards in Saigon, that's who I'm talking about." He drove faster, had passed the ammo dump and the mortar pit already, heading out to the perimeter road.

"They push a goddamn pin in a map," Command said, "and that's it. To them, that's all this is."

"I've had that thought myself, sometimes, sir."

"Sergeant, when it's time for you to bitch, I'll tell you," Command said. Then smiled at him. "The old man needs to let off steam." They passed Tower Nine, and up there, Lemmen thought he could see the reflection of Arvin faces and eyes.

"Oh, I imagine, Sergeant, some people might think the world is all satisfaction to a man of rank—but it just ain't so. What the hell have I done since I got this command, but lie and be lied to?"

He stopped the jeep. They were at the far south corner of the base, just near the control tower. Blue lights glowed on the runway, some of them burnt out now. Command shut off the engine. Got out of the jeep. Far away there were two explosions, one right after the other. He looked toward Can Tho. "Well," he said, drawing the word out. He put his hands in his back pocket. "Guess we've about shot the rapids."

Neither of them said anything for a while. Command

took off his cap, ran his hand over his gray hair, put his cap back on. "You and me, Sergeant," Command said finally.

"Sir?"

"Forget Fort Carson. I ripped those orders up the day I gave 'em to you. You're going to be my aide in Saigon. Clean up the paperwork mess and that kind of thing. You're a lucky man. I wouldn't want to be down here if Charley comes through." He got behind the wheel of the jeep. "Let's go."

Lemmen got in. They rode in bumpy silence over a grass strip and over the runway; didn't stop until they were back at the trailer. Command pulled the emergency brake, got out, went up the steps and inside, and in a moment he was back, throwing two American Tourister suitcases into the back of the jeep.

"We're going now?" Lemmen said. "By jeep?"

"They ain't going to send Air Force One after us," Command said. He laughed at his own joke, got behind the wheel. "We'll both be doing KP unless we get up there by first light."

Lemmen thought quick. "I'd like to stop by the bunker and get a few of my things."

Command said nothing, just drove the jeep around the corner. Lemmen thought he and Hoa would just sneak out the back door, hide until Command drove away; then he reconsidered. The honest approach might work.

"Would it be possible," Lemmen said, "to take a couple of nationals with us, sir?"

"Nationals? You mean Captain Loan? Why, that coward son of a bitch, let him rot here where he belongs. I'm asking Colonel Tho to transfer him right back to the Cambodian border."

"What I meant really," Lemmen said, "was to take an orphan boy I know, and this girlfriend of mine, well, actually, you know her pretty well, it's Hoa, sir."

"Hoa?" Command said. He took his eyes away from the

road and looked at Lemmen. Then a slow look of comprehension made its way across his face. He smiled. "You and Hoa?"

"That's right, sir."

"I'll be damned," Command said, and grinned. "Right under my damn nose."

Lemmen didn't say anything for a moment.

"She's a damn fine woman, Sergeant. Full of spunk. Mite skinny, but just full of spunk. She's done a fine job for me—but I'll tell you what. There ain't a bit of room in here for her."

"She can sit on my lap, sir."

"What about the boy?" Command said, "No, Sergeant, we can't risk it. We'll be going up the road, it'll be all dark, I can't take a boy and a woman along on a combat mission. There'd be hell to pay if they got hurt. No. Maybe they can come up later—bring them up in the daytime. But where are they going to stay, Sergeant? Saigon is loaded with refugees."

He stopped the jeep at the barracks door. Idled it. "Hurry and get your things, Sergeant."

Lemmen got out of the jeep. Saluted. "I'm not going, sir," he said.

"Sergeant Lemmen," Command said. "I don't know what's got into you but I'm giving you a direct order to get your weapon and one bag of your belongings and get back in this jeep double time."

"Not going, sir."

Command got out of the jeep. Stood face-to-face with Lemmen. "Now look here. You're going to ride shotgun with me to Saigon, and when we get there, what you do is your business the rest of the day. You can have the jeep. If you want to turn around and come back here to pick up your girlfriend, as long as I didn't authorize it, why, I don't give a damn."

Lemmen thought for a moment. The jeep! Of course. Why hadn't he thought of that? He could drive back here in an hour—two at most. Then they could go anywhere. Drive to the coast. A few hours in Saigon wouldn't hurt anything. Maybe he could get some money out of the Red Cross. He would hear all the latest rumors. He could ask around about ship captains. Payday coming, too. If nothing else worked, he could sell the jeep for airfare. Or drive Hoa and Van out to Vung Tau himself, get in line with the refugees.

"I can have the jeep and turn around as soon as we make Saigon? Do I have your word, sir?"

"You've got it," Command said.

Lemmen stepped back and saluted. "Double time, sir," he said, and turned for the barracks. Ran down the hall to his room. Hoa was sleeping, candle still burning, radios still crackling. He grabbed his carbine, turned off the radios, bent down to Hoa. Kissed her on the lips. "I'll be back in a couple of hours," he said.

She rolled on her side. She did not seem fully awake.

"Where are you going?" she mumbled.

"Sleep, I'll be back," he said, and caressed her face. She groaned. She did not open her eyes. He snuffed out the candle just as Command sounded the horn.

"Wait for me," he said, and fumbled in the dark for his carbine, backed out the door, blew her a kiss, let the door shut, ran past the sleeping wives, children, soldiers, out into the night.

"Your bag," Command said.

"I'll come back for it."

Command put the jeep in gear. "Lock and load, Sergeant, we're not going to meet anybody friendly, this time of night." He got the jeep rolling toward the main gate. The two Arvin sentries saluted and the major drove by them, took a left on Route 4, stepped hard on the gas. Lemmen drew a deep breath of that grassy night aroma that would always remind him of this beautiful country; then he turned in his seat and looked back.